Other Collections by J. Daniel Sawyer

Sculpting God: Bedtime Stories for Adults
Frock Coat Dreams: Romances, Nightmares, and Fancies from the
Steampunk Fringe

Other Fiction by J. Daniel Sawyer

Down From Ten
Ideas, Inc.
The Resurrection Junket
Hadrian's Flight

The Clarke Lantham Mysteries
And Then She Was Gone
A Ghostly Christmas Present
Smoke Rings Silent Victor
He Ain't Heavy
In The Cloud
Blood and Weeds
The Bodies In The Basement
The Sky Miners (forthcoming)

Suave Rob's Awesome Adventures!
Suave Rob's Double-X Derring-Do
Suave Rob's Rough-n-Ready Rugrat Rapture
Suave Rob's Amazing Ass-Saving Association (forthcoming)

coming soon: *The Kabrakan Ascendency*
The Briggs Defection
The Orinthal Deception
The Hartman Gambit
The Reeves Directive
The Singh Hegemony
The Mannix Initiative

For news, updates, and new releases,
sign up for J. Daniel Sawyer's newsletter at www.jdsawyer.net

Tales of a Lombard Alchemist: Volume 1

AWP Fantasty, a division of ArtisticWhispers Productions, Inc.
Copyright © 2017 J. Daniel Sawyer
All Rights Reserved

Book Design by ArtisticWhispers
Cover art *City at the Edge of Nowhere* © 2017 Kitty NicIaian
All rights reserved. Used with permission.

At the Edge of Nowhere © 2011
The Empty House © 2015
Sunday Morning Giraffe © 2012
Chicken Noodle Gravity © 2011
Funeral Hats © 2016
Pick a Card © 2017
The Serpent and the Satchel © 2012

Publishers Note:

Tales of the Lombard Alchemist

Volume 1

J. Daniel Sawyer

TALES

INTRODUCTION

HIGH IN THE DESERT, between the mountains out west, up where the ground throbs from the nuclear test detonations, the casinos still glitter. But the city around them has cracked and dried, like the edges of a scab on the verge of infection.

But the casinos still draw them. People from the far reaches of the world come here to try their luck, to take a chance, to have the adventures they wouldn't write home about.

And sometimes they run out of luck, with nowhere left to turn, no money, no options, no hope, and no clue.

When you fall that low, you need that one special thing that might change everything.

I know. I can smell them. They find me in the old pawn shop in the hot zone in this broken-down gambling town at the edge of nowhere. And, for a price, I can provide what they need.

Sometimes they buy.

Sometimes they sell.

And sometimes...they stay.

At The Edge of Nowhere

SOMETIMES YOU MOVE because you want to. Sometimes, you move because you have to.

I had to.

So I found a place in a two-floor walk-up in a city just this side of nowhere.

A way to get lost?

To get lost, you have to know where you're at to start with. All I knew is what I was leaving, and that I had three weeks of cash float to find a job.

Nobody was hiring in any field I knew anything about—granted, that wasn't a lot. At nineteen, I'd done more than most people ten years older than me, but I was nineteen, and there's only so much you learn by that time.

Quick as bread goes stale, I ran through my prospects. By the end of five weeks, I was down to pocket money, and only got that by selling bits of junk I found on the street to make me last a little longer. Even then, I was running out of places to sell. Even in a city full of gamblers, there are only so many pawn shops, recycling centers, and used bookstores. When that's all you've got to make it on, and you're a kid that pushes too hard, you use up good will fast.

Mine was pretty much gone.

You find yourself in situations like that when you grow up being taught that money isn't important as long as you're a good person. If I learned anything in those three weeks, it's that when you don't have enough money to eat and sleep, you don't stay a good person for long. Even in that economy, there was plenty of work for someone willing to look the other way.

One thing about being on the edge of nowhere: "looking the other way" doesn't mean ignoring a buddy stealing pencils from the company store. There was one night I got cold and hungry enough I actually went down to 43rd street, where the streetwalkers do their thing, to talk to a pimp about a bodyguard job. He assigned me to a twelve year old—couldn't tell if it was a girl or a boy dressing cross, but it didn't matter. Without money to get back across town to my rooms, I didn't have much choice; I slept under the bridge with a rock in my hand and nothing but air in my belly.

But by morning, I knew that if I didn't find some way to turn a buck, I'd be back to the pimp tonight, and I'd protect the customer from that twelve-year-old if the kid tried to bite, and I'd do it with a smile.

Some people say you've always got a choice. Those people have never made so many wrong ones that the choices start making themselves.

I had the jacket on my back—the last bit of home I still owned. I'd have to sell it to eat, and to get a bus ticket.

There was only one place near here I could maybe trade it for a few bits—the one hock house left in town that I'd not hit yet. Time to time I heard about it from other drifters while diving in dumpsters for the occasional treasure someone tossed away, but I'd never gone. Too far past the end of the bus line, too expensive to make the trip.

Two miles of walk. I still had enough rubber on the bottoms of my shoes to make that.

One mile along, it started to rain, and hard.

A little gray bungalow at the end of town, used to be a family house back in the days when families didn't mind living this far from the good schools—back when most people were farmers and laborers. Now it was just a shop, the front walls knocked out so the windows could be expanded, the plate glass providing no view past the cram-and-crush of trinkets and junk.

There were a lot of dollar signs. I remember the way they looked, lit through the rain like the yellow lamps on the bow of a ship coming through the fog to rescue folks off a shipwreck.

Word on the street was they paid well—I'd have been happy if they paid enough for a hamburger.

The door had a bell, like you might hear in a Christmas tune. Ghoulish, ringing as I stepped through the door to look directly into the dead

eyes of a stuffed creature I couldn't quite identify. A badger? A wolverine? Whatever it was,
it looked like it was having the kind of day I was. I
shied away, skulking along one of the display cases,
taking in the gaudy jewelry, the antique stamps, the
crosses and pentacles, the pearl-handled revolvers.
Nothing had a price tag, but any one of the things
here would have fed me for a week. Maybe two.
Not even the foreigner at the high-end hock shop
downtown would turn one of these things away.

It was all locked away under glass. I couldn't
get to it if I tried without making a god-awful row.
I hadn't had a chance to learn to pick a lock, and,
pathetic as it sounds, I shied from breaking the
glass mostly because I couldn't afford band-aids
for my hands.

That point when choices make themselves? I
was past that, to the point where the choices make
you.

To get into the display cases I'd need a key. To
get out of town, I needed someone willing to loan
me five on the jacket.

But the shop was empty—not a soul, not a
whisper except for my own breathing.

"Hello?" I don't really know how loud I said it.
In that moment, I didn't really want an answer. If
nobody was there, perhaps I could stay out of the
rain for a few minutes. Perhaps I could look longer.

There was a fire at one end of the room, in
a fireplace left over from when the shop was a
home. A family lived here once. Probably the

showroom used to be bedrooms and a family room. Maybe they watched TV right where I was standing. Maybe they yelled at their children about the company they kept. Maybe one of them beat another to a pulp in this room over some small thing—a hairbrush left out of place, or a failure to wash the dishes, or a skirmish over bed times.

The possibilities were cold as the room. The merest hint of breath fogged in front of my face—the fire didn't seem anything more than a light show, even when I walked close. I was soaked to the skin, and shivering. Drawing my jacket around me for the last few minutes of our relationship was like making love to a girl you plan on leaving—the touch was nothing more than a reminder of the sheer uselessness.

And like a useless woman, it only left me colder.

I could have used some of this cold last night. Qualms felt warm—but without them, I wouldn't be starving now, and freezing. I'd have a meal and a bath and be home in my bed, such as it was. At least for today.

The mantelpiece was festooned with taxidermy over the cold-enough-to-be-dead-fire; all manner of birds and vermin. If I brushed them aside, would I see a device for calling up demons? Why else would a fire be so cold?

Or maybe it was just me.

I tapped at the different trophies. Light and hollow, stuffed with sawdust, nothing remarkable about them, other than their deadness.

But as they shifted around, I spotted something between—a watch, white gold, but thick with dust. In a clean room. This must have been forgotten behind the trophies for years. Completely neglected, on a silver fob. Old. The mechanism still worked when I wound it. Might fetch a few hundred on the open market.

My fingers twitched against the hearth's oak. Somehow, sinking to theft felt lower than the job I'd turned down last night.

But that was last night, and this was today. My mouth watered as my tongue curled around the pizza it would taste once I hocked the watch uptown. My spine shivered even more as my gooseflesh imagined a weatherproof coat to see me through the winter. Every nerve stood on the brink of action. It was, after all, a forgotten thing.

It wouldn't be missed.

"May I help you?" hacked a voice behind me.

I nearly jumped out of my skin. Every hair on my body stood on end, and my heart, for just a moment, stopped. I could feel eyes boring into the back of my head, and a labored breathing. Somewhere in the excitement, I yanked my hand back from a hearth, like a child caught near the cookie jar prepping for a snatch-and-grab.

"Oh. Um. I think so." I turned, hiding my right hand behind my body, and slipped the watch into my jeans pocket on top of my wallet. Instinct.

"Please, come over here. Come into the light.

My eyes aren't what they used to be."

He stood behind the counter furthest from the door, his hands resting on the display case that contained the weapons. His eyes sank back into his skull like they'd seen too much and were retreating, but slowly, so the rest of him wouldn't notice.

My eyes felt like that sometimes.

Like the rest of me, they were out of places to run.

"So, my boy, what would you like to buy?"

"Oh, nothing. I'm just looking. This your place?"

"Mmm. Been here most sixty years. Started off with bubblegum and baseball cards, sweeping up after hours."

"Long time."

"When a man's life finds him, he listens," the old man swept his arm out to indicate all the items on display in the showroom. "Wonders from all corners of the world—exotic species now extinct, preserved on our walls for generations to come." It was a carnival barker's speech, like the I'd heard from the guy in front of the strip club on 50th. Even through the cracked leather of his vocal chords, he had me by the end of the first sentence. "Weapons that once rested in the hands of Al Capone, or Calamity Jane. See anything you like?"

"All of it. It's great." I looked around again as it occurred to me that every piece here was something this man bought. A lifetime's worth of collecting, of short swap deals, of curiosities and secrets, all hanging on the walls in here. For some reason, walking around inside a man's soul like this made my stomach quaver. That, and the water sliding from my soaked collar down my spine, made me reconsider. Creep city. "I'm sorry, I've made a mistake, I...I don't have any money. Didn't mean to bother you."

I turned to go. A California Grizzly, claws at the ready, stood between me and the door. For a second, I was sure I could see its breath puffing in front of its face. Which was nonsense. Of course it was. It was a stuffed specimen of an extinct species.

"If you weren't intending to buy, perhaps you have something you would like to sell?"

"I wish." I didn't quite have the courage to look him in the eye. Instead, I took my lapels in my fingers and held the jacket open, then turned around as if to prove I wasn't carrying a weapon. "This is everything I've got."

"Perhaps there is more value there than you believe."

The watch felt hot against my hip, as if his gaze could set it alight.

"Maybe," I said. "But I'll keep it for now."

I ZIPPED UP my soaked jacket and scurried out, like a rat eager to hide a morsel of cheese from peering eyes. Another week—maybe two—to find work. Work I could be proud to do. Work that would keep me fed. Work that would let me sleep at night without having to re-live every moment of my day.

Some kind of dignity, and who gave a damn that I bought it with a little theft? Better that than the alternative.

Besides, no one would miss the watch. No one even knew it was there.

AT THE BUS STOP, I ran face-first into my folly. I had not pawned the jacket. I had not sold it. I was just as cash-poor as I'd been when I found the last hock shop in town. No way home, except to hoof it—that meant crossing through the Forgotten district. Without a weapon. Again.

The pavement was turning icy. The rain pelting me in the face froze solid as soon as it hit. If ever there was a hell to find on earth, this surely was the place. With treasure in my pocket that I couldn't sell, I turned left on Southfork and trudged toward 43rd. The pimps were open twenty-four seven.

I went back to the one who offered me the job last night—still on duty, minding his market. A run-down storefront with apartments above for the knocking shop. Streetwalkers out front, all dressed like various flavors of decay.

I told him I needed quick cash. The man said fifteen dollars. For only an hour. All I had to do was stand there in the ratty upstairs room, make sure the merchandise behaved itself. Make sure the customer didn't damage it.

That's what he called the kid too: merchandise.

The customer was a couple. They worked in shifts. First her. Then him. Then her again. Making it into a seduction. Pretending it was a romance.

Making the kid watch while they did their thing with each other, then putting the kid in the middle.

I had the easy chair near the door, made sure they couldn't leave if things got ugly.

Ugly, you can guess, was a relative term.

As for the kid? I didn't even see its face. Didn't know if it was a boy or a girl. All I knew was it was a piece of four-foot-three mobile entertainment, and as long as it was just a collection of sounds, it wasn't real.

But as the customers played out their script like a staged ballet, they didn't think about the wallets they left on the bureau. In arm's reach. With seventy dollars between them.

I closed the door so softly, not even a dog could've heard it. I tiptoed to the back of the building. I ducked out the window and slid as quick as I could down the fire escape.

The alley opened halfway between 43rd and 44th. I headed uptown, toward the bus stop on 46th and waited for the coach to take me home. The bench had a little shelter over it, which gave me meager—but welcome—protection from the wind.

Out here in the high desert—dry because the ground sucked the water away, not because it didn't fall—the wind has its own voice; a hollow drone moaning songs that, before I came here, I only heard when I was half-asleep and alone. The kind of sound you don't like to remember, and it beat against the bus stop walls on a day already full of sounds that, no matter how long I lived or how many drugs I took, I'd never be able to stop hearing.

Another young man joined me, huddling up against the opposite corner like my stunt double. He looked like I felt. We waited together for a minute or two, mirrors of desolation. A bus came, but it was the wrong line—heading out of town to the north—so it left without interrupting our silent understanding. He lit a cigarette and blew it out into the comparatively still air between us. I matched it with puffs of cold fog.

To his credit, my companion gave me several warnings like that in the five minutes we shared, but I was still new to this side of life. I hadn't learned the language of looks that gives you a second chance to come clean, or to step on the wrong bus while there was still time.

He finished his cigarette and produced another. After fumbling with his chintzy convenience store lighter he looked at me like a man who'd gone too long between meals.

"'Scuse me, Mister, could ya...my fingers are all froze and I gots ta..."

"Yeah. Yeah, sure." My fingers, until recently happy and warm in my pocket wrapped around the watch, took the lighter from him and struck a flame while the wind whipped past. I held it up, shielding it as best I could with my colder hand.

"Thanks." He pushed his face toward the flame, rested his left hand on my wrist, and stepped toward me.

Then, there was pain. The most exquisite pain, like good liquor, a kind of burning cold that seemed to slide forever until it pierced my heart. Then it was gone again.

The world, wrapped in the sound of wind, tumbled up to meet me. The concrete floor of the bus stop seemed much more intense viewed side-on, with all its little pebbles and perturbations. Like frozen waves on an unnoticed sea.

His hands patted my pockets, found the wad of cash in the back one, and took it. I didn't see where he went.

I must have thrashed around. I might have tried to call for help, but really, with so little breath, in wind that was so loud, there was no way anyone could have heard. All I could hear was ticking.

When life flows out of you onto that placid, frozen concrete sea, it passes through a kind of lens, and everything focuses. You figure out what's really important, and maybe it's not too late. I knew that I could do something that would make all the difference. Leave some mark on history; a coffee stain on a forgotten page, instead of just a finger smudge. I could make sure the clock was right.

My fingers didn't want to work right. It seemed to take an hour to fumble the fob out of my pocket. The watch splashed in the red river, open. I batted at it, managed to get the little knob up where it spun freely. It was off. The time was wrong. It didn't match the clock on the bank across the street.

A last swing, my arm landed on the watch, and the world melted like wax on a hot rock...

"FIFTEEN FOR THE HOUR." The pimp's book-keeper, a small man with metal teeth, nodded past me to the brothel waiting room.

A couple, beautiful and well turned out like you might see in any advertisement, looked through a picture-book of prepubescents as if they were here to adopt. They lingered and cooed over some, sharing secret looks and laughter.

My right hip pocket was warm—warmer than I remembered. Not enough to burn, but enough to make me itch.

"Room 315."

I nodded and took the money and the room key. The couple made their selection and asked for directions. I escorted them halfway up the first flight of stairs, then stopped. "I just remembered, something I gotta do. Here." I mumbled and handed them the room key. "The...merchandise will be in the foyer on the second floor. Um...excuse me."

I hurried back down the stairs and threw my fifteen bucks down on the bookkeeper's desk. I ran out, chased by a stream of invective. There had to be another way to make bus fare.

Still soaked to the skin. When I hit the freezing air on the stoop I almost went back inside. Wind like a knife between my ribs—a feeling I knew I could remember, though I wasn't sure how. I took two, maybe three breaths, before the enforcers burst open the door behind me.

Nobody backs out once they've been paid.

I ran. On no food and less sleep, I ran while the icy air scorched my lungs. Water ran in my mouth like it did in the gutters. My feet slipped every which way as they strained for the vanishing traces of grip between patches of ice.

One intersection passed.

Two.

Three.

Nothing else mattered but keeping my footing.

The park. The park would hide me. A chance glance back showed me they were trapped behind fast-flowing traffic one street back. I heard a bus.

Of course! A bus. It would hide me.

Diesel-powered salvation.

Except I couldn't afford to get on. They'd throw me off to die at the hands of the animals I almost joined.

Crushed between the bus and the park, I dove over the low cobble wall and scurried under the bush into a mud hole. Thirty seconds later, two Chicanos and a harried albino leaped the wall and stopped, mere yards from my burrow.

The rest of the park was a lawn, open as a baby's face.

My pocket burned. The only place on my whole body that knew even the memory of warmth.

I fumbled the fob out. I wanted to watch the last seconds I'd have as a human—if I was really human anymore.

But it had stopped. Footsteps round the bush I was under, and the watch had stopped. I wound and wound and wound until it wouldn't click anymore. What time was it?

Two boots tramped in front of me.

"Oho! Lookie here! I found me a sewer rat." More clicks, but these came from above me. "I say we leave him for the cats."

I'd never heard a bang that loud. I didn't know what to make of the hole in my hand. I didn't know why my vision went dark. The cold taking my brain. At least the watch was warm. Warm enough even to melt the world again...

"If you weren't intending to buy, perhaps you have something you would like to sell?" The old man behind the counter held a cat. I didn't remember a cat, but there it was. He kneaded its head right between the ears.

I couldn't quite bring myself to look him in the eye, but I looked everywhere else. The fire still burned without heat. The breath still fogged in front of my face. The hock shop's walls, still festooned with every artifact of nightmare I could dream up.

"I...don't I wish." I took my lapels in my fingers and had held the jacket open, then turned a full circle on the spot as if to prove I wasn't carrying a weapon. "This is everything I've got."

"Perhaps there is more value there than you believe."

The watch burned against my hip, so hot I could swear I smelled my flesh roasting. Like a rodent gnawing through to my bones, and yet I somehow managed not to scream. "Maybe. But I'll keep it for now."

I zipped up my soaked jacket and scurried out into the freezing rain. But three steps out the door I remembered the bus fare. I needed a way to get back to the other pawn shops if I was going to sell the watch. Something—I can't call it memory and still be truthful, but an awareness, perhaps—drove me back into the shop.

But the man was gone.

A bell sat on the display case next to a statue of a Hindu idol.

I rang it, then looked over the display cases again. Anything in here—even the stamps, even the baseball cards, would be enough to buy me breakfast if I could get back across town. I needed *something*.

My hip kept burning. My ribs ached. My hand hurt. Like I was riddled with the holes of forgotten violence. I rubbed the pocket where the stolen watch sat.

"Did you forget something?" The man didn't have a cat this time.

"I...uh...no. Just..." I held the lapels of my bomber jacket again. "How much for this?"

"Put it here." He tapped the display case.

I shucked the battered, stained thing that used to be suede, and laid it before him for judgment.

"Not good condition, no no no." He fretted over it. He found holes in it. "Blood stains, my my. Fresh too. You're lucky to be alive."

I couldn't see it when I was wearing it, but the front was saturated with tacky blood.

His fingers worked through several holes. Some from water damage. One that looked like a knife. When he fingered it, my ribs tickled.

He pressed the neck liner to his nose and inhaled. "Smells of old sin. Come now, my lad, do you think you can change your fate by changing your clothes? No, no, this won't do at all." He fretted over it some more, ran his fingers over every inch as if he could read my past from it. "Rough. Shattered plans, my my. It does have a tale to tell, doesn't it. Tell me, how did you come here?"

"I just..." I realized I couldn't remember. There was last night under the bridge, hoping no one would find me. And there was this morning in the rain. And running from the pimp's men. And watching the couple with their hired child. And memories of blood and melting wax. I rubbed at the heat in my jeans, like I was aroused and embarrassed. "I don't remember. I just need to get home."

"Home," he said, "Is a dream. Just a dream. Nothing more. A lie we soothe with, a fairy tale for wounds too fresh. No, no, this won't do at all. I can't do anything with it."

He pushed the jacket back to me. "There's nothing of value here. Do you have anything else?"

I rubbed my pocket. My stomach twisted around its lack of food. Something in the middle of my body shivered, as if I'd been sliced open at the crotch by an icicle. I had to find some kind of warmth, some kind of food. I needed money, and fast.

"No. Nothing. Just a wallet. Just my clothes. Please," All these weeks, I'd managed not to beg. I'd never begged anyone for anything. "Please, you have to help me. I can't go back out there. I'll die. I don't have anything left. I spent it all. I don't have anywhere else to go. Don't make me go." I clutched my arms and rubbed them fast, trying to bring back some kind of heat.

The felt like ice.

They felt like death.

"Please, I can't go."

"No," he said. His voice calm, like the sound of war just before it starts. "No, you cannot go out there." He looked into my eyes. I avoided it, concentrated on finding a way back into my jacket, even though it was colder and dirtier than I was.

I rubbed the searing pocket again. "Tell me, son, what is in your pocket?"

"Nothing. I'm sorry. I shouldn't have come." I turned away and plunged to the door to take my chances in the cold.

"You cannot leave," he said from behind me.

I opened the door and tried to step out, but something held me back. Not reluctance. More like someone had strung a rope around my neck. Every time I tried to step, it got tighter, until I had to back off into the shadow of the ravening wolverine.

"It is not safe out there."

"No...no, I'm sorry, I have to go."

"But you can't." The cat perched on his shoulder like a vulture. It rode the man while he walked toward me, as if approaching a new trophy. Sizing me up. Deciding where I belonged.

"I...I can't. Why?" I rubbed furiously at the watch. All heat. All burning. No warmth. If I burst into flames I'd never feel warm again. "I don't understand."

"But you do. Are you sure there is nothing else of value you have?"

"I'm sure."

"Pity. Such a waste. But this," he dipped into my pocket and retrieved the stolen watch, "belongs in the case." He retreated behind the counter again and rang up the watch. "There's an outstanding balance. Interest against a loan. Have you nothing to pay it off?"

"This is everything I have."

"Then I suppose," he said, "It will have to do."

ON THE EDGE OF NOWHERE, between the city and the abandoned suburbs, a small bungalow used to house a family. Now, it houses treasures, all of them once considered too dear to part with. And the shopkeeper gives loans on dreams that can't pay their own way. Sometimes he buys, sometimes he sells. Like everyone else in town, he deals in chance. In my case, three chances.

All my life, I heard people say you make your own choices. Maybe that's true. Maybe most people never get to the point where choices make themselves. Fewer still, to the point where the choices make *them*. But I did.

Turns out I did have something of value to sell. Like the rest of the things in the shop, it's a trophy now, as much as the stuffed bear, or the wolverine. It's the man behind the counter, who trades in wishes and needs. A young man, with the bullet wound on the back of his hand. A solitary man, working in the house that used to be a home, by the fire that gives no heat, who can never leave.

I don't own him anymore.

He's just interest on the loan.

THE EMPTY HOUSE

for Steena

IN THE END, LONELINESS was the real problem. Normally, one doesn't think of a house as being lonely, unless perhaps it sits on the crown of a remote mountain. Normally, houses can't *be* lonely. Then again, houses aren't normally hand-built by Alan Tosetti, and most houses that he built weren't left unfinished when he keeled over in the middle of shaping the edge molding on the mantelpiece, or occupied in their unfinished state by his grieving daughter who was convinced that his spirit somehow lived on in the timbers.

None of those things could really explain what happened in there, though. Not on their own. And it didn't explain why nobody in the neighborhood dared speak of it anymore. For the house truly *was* lonely, and the gnawing emptiness at its core had sent one occupant after another to the hospital, the asylum, or the grave with symptoms that nobody had ever seen before.

Tosetti's youngest daughter, for example, died sitting in her chair in front of that mantelpiece, stroking a hat that had once belonged to her father.

She died six months after moving in, on her twenty-sixth birthday.

She died of old age.

She wasn't the last.

IN HIS HEYDAY–SEVENTY years ago—Alan Tosetti was the sterling standard in a town built on silver. He designed the first casino here. He built the suburbs, the vast tracts of housing from the town's silver age, before the bomb tests turned his developments into a hot zone.

But Tosetti's passion wasn't housing, or architecture, or building, or even carpentry, it was the wood. He loved wood in the same way a medium loves the dead—the ridges of the grain against the pads of his fingers whispered the variety, the history, the story of any wood in a language only he could understand.

His passion began in his childhood, when he murdered his first lover: a tall oak that grew in his back yard. A tree he'd climbed, and built clubhouses in, and swooped from on rope swings since he first could walk. He used an axe, and then a pit saw, and dismembered her body. Then he used chisels and sanders to re-shape her flesh into a table and a chest of drawers. From that day forward, he found himself unable to resist the beautiful corpses of generations-old trees. He coveted their hearts, he longed for their flesh, he devoted his life to molding them into visions of perfection.

Odd, perhaps, that a man so consumed would chose to build a city in the high desert, but his journals—which found their way into the shop upon his death—told the truth about that, as they did about everything else. He learned architecture (and built this town) because, in this climate, wood lasts forever. It was a monument to his lovers, their bodies on display in a perfect mausoleum. A gift to the ages: beauty, perfectly preserved.

When the bomb tests blew their radioactive winds through his precious development, it left his legacy in ruins. It was now a hot zone, they said, unfit for human habitation for the next hundred years. The desert reclaimed the homes the people fled, the churches that stood silent, the libraries with silent towers of books perched carefully on the gorgeous inlaid shelves capped with bas reliefs designed and crafted by Alan Tosetti and his apprentices. The buildings his daughter watched him build from the safety of her pram.

Sixty years old, time to start nearly from scratch? It might have ruined lesser man.

Not Tosetti.

He turned his attention to custom homes. The town, he decided, needed a history. Victorians, and Tudors, and Craftsmen homes in all styles, all sizes. Each unique. Each built with materials and methods appropriate to the original period. He'd build them to last five hundred years or more.

And build them he did. At lavish expense, he cobbled together edifices the likes of which his generation had never seen.

His quest eventually brought him to us.

He wanted mahogany, a variety that he couldn't import. He said we owed him—he built the house which was now our shop. We—the royal we, meaning the words the Shopkeeper before me was authorized to utter by the Master of the shop—found it expedient to agree rather than pointing out that our presence was the only thing that kept any of his precious creation from being looted or falling over dead from decay.

The Master had Its reasons, and my predecessor did not interfere. Once I became part of the institutional Memory, I also learned not to interfere. My incarceration was more bearable that way. And according to the Book of Law, interference incurred penalties that would extend my sentence. In here, everyone must pay for their sins.

According to the Memory, when Tosetti came to us, the Master deemed it appropriate to sell him the mahogany salvaged from the floor of the Lutheran church in the hot zone—the church that Tosetti himself had built.

"It has to be perfect," he said. "I will pay any price you set."

He had done business with us before. He knew what he was saying. Maybe he even knew what that wood would do to that house—maybe it was the reason he wanted it; to give the house a truly enchanted finish.

He took the mahogany back to his masterwork

and re-milled it. He laid it down on the parlor floor and tacked it in by hand. He used hand tools to join the oak core to the mahogany veneer on the coffee table. He chiseled the edge of the fireplace mantle by hand, and that's when he died. Maybe the house decided it wanted him too much to let him go.

Whatever the reason, the house took him, and his eldest daughter inherited it. She managed to pay us off, so the house lived on, and, as far as the Master was concerned, it ceased to exist. The Shopkeeper, though, did care. Tosetti was the man he'd wanted to be, back before he'd earned his sentence here, so he kept clippings. Every news story that ran about Tosetti made its way into a battered leather scrapbook in the office—when you're incarcerated, you read everything you can. The Master didn't mind what I did, so long as I obeyed the rules: serve the customer, satisfy their desires, and mercilessly enforce every contract.

TOSETTI'S DAUGHTER BROUGHT HIS ashes back to that house and perched them on that mantle. She wiped out her trust fund to pay off his debts, but she was determined to finish his monument. Nobody seemed surprised—mad, irascible, unpleasant genius he may have been, but somehow he made everyone love him. Viewing the Memory, it didn't surprise me. Standing across the counter from him was like being in the presence of an Olympian god. Something in his aura made you want to love him, made you want to prostrate yourself before him, to beg him to give you the ultimate pleasure, to use you for his greatness. Like the Master, but without the terror.

She loved him. She poured her life into his last legacy. She found the finest antiquities for it, she hired the finest tradesmen to put the finish on Tosetti's work, she furnished it in precise style: Arts and Crafts furniture for the finest Craftsman ever built. She told the reporters that she owed it to his memory.

And two years later when her debt was paid, and the second floor was finished, she married the carpenter who managed the job. After their honeymoon, her husband carried her over the threshold, and they lit a fire under the very hearth her father had given his life for, and the two of them laid naked on the bearskin rug, and they claimed the house with their lovemaking.

A delivery boy found them like that, a week later, both naked and sallow and still joined together, their faces twisted in ecstasy, their skin marred by the teeth marks of vermin that lived beneath the house. The house had reclaimed its own.

Her younger sister came next. Taking her place in the house, one night—so the story goes—she found a box containing her father's old clothes. She sat down with his hat to watch the fire, and lost herself to time. Nobody could explain how a woman so young could have such thin white hair, such frail, papery hands, such exhausted sweetness in her ash-gray face as she did when a church friend found her mummified body some weeks later.

The next owner was Tosetti's long lost son. It took a year to locate him, a professor in his mid-forties living in England, and he ordered the place locked up until he decided how to dispense with it. Twenty years later, he returned—widowed and childless and in his dotage—to claim his inheritance. He brought with him the legacy of a lifetime spent in Oxfordshire; books and paintings and sculptures and mementos. Two months later, the neighbors found him pacing the front yard at night, foaming at the mouth, raving, naked. When the medics managed to get a response out of him, he muttered: "They all were fools. All fools, God help them. She hated them, hated them, hated them, the poor fools." Consensus grew in the neighborhood that his mind had broken from living in the house where his father and sisters had all died.

Over the next few years, the house passed from hand to hand. A family moved in and quickly moved out again, claiming it was haunted. They sued to get out of their mortgage. They lost the case, so they defaulted. The bank took it into receivership, then a group of local history enthusiasts sued the bank to get the house donated to the city as a heritage site.

For years, nobody lived there. Nobody breathed there. Nobody loved there. The magnificent place gathered cobwebs and desert dust and weathering, and it waited. The longing, hungering, empty ache settled in on its timbers like snow on the limbs of an old willow, with no one the wiser. And time wore on, even still.

When finally the machinery of government wound through, and the bribes were paid, and the appointments made, the deed to the house finally vested in a trust set up for that house alone, the doors opened again for the first time in twenty-eight years, and a person walked inside.

One person only.

He looked around, shivered. Then he came to me.

"Look," he said, "the place is filled with crap I can't begin to identify. Expensive crap, and I've got to bring it back up to original condition, just the way Tosetti left it. I know there's stuff there you'll want. But I need a truck, and no one around here hires trucks anymore." He called himself "Campbell," dressed for the spring weather outside and shivered in the corpse-cold shop air, but it didn't hold him back. He was thirty-five, maybe forty years old, and not someone used to taking no for an answer.

I spread my hands, palms-up, over the glass counter. "I'm sorry sir, but I can't help you. We don't hire vehicles here. What you see, we have to sell. What you bring, we sometimes buy. If it's valuable, we can maybe make you a loan. But I'm not in the rental business."

"Well, can you at least come take a look? Tell me if there's anything you want?"

"Why would you want me?"

"You pay the best rates, or so they say. We can make a deal—I just need to clean it up so I can...well, no reason not to tell you. Look, I've been stuck in this goddamn town for four years, and this is my ticket out. I get this place set up nice, and find a good caretaker, and I can pull up stakes and get back to civilization. See the folks back home, knowing I've done some good. There's a girl back there, she's waiting for me. I'd like to go back with my head high and my pockets full, you follow?"

I chewed my lip. In my days before the pawnshop, I'd walked past Tosetti's last house as I searched for work, or food, or some bit of trash I could sell. Anything to get on another day.

But I never went in.

Coming to this city on the edge of nowhere had been a mistake. Everyone who lives here could probably say the same thing. You get a feel for a city when you spend enough time on its streets. You learn how to tell when not to ask questions. Little things: rubber scuff marks on the door jamb and the floor; lawn mowed, but flower beds un-weeded; a stray corner of mail sticking just barely out of the mail slot, its edges yellowed with age. The kind of fallow place where druggies broke in to do their thing. The kind of place where people like the man I used to be would get eaten for lunch.

And, like Campbell, I'd do just about anything

to get out of this town.

"I'm sorry," I said, "But I can't..."

Before I could finish, the Master leapt up onto the counter between us and nuzzled Campbell with Its bald, wrinkled head. It then turned to me and meowed, tilted Its nose up and licked Campbell's patting hand.

"He seems to think you should."

"I'm sorry, sir, but we just don't have the..."

The Master interrupted me again, leaping onto my upper arm and climbing onto my shoulders, claws out. It stropped back and forth behind my head, digging in and drawing blood under my thick felt sportcoat every time a paw touched me.

"Mroooow," It said. And in the back of my head I heard Its cold, thin voice: *Accommodate him.*

I did not know what might happen if I disobeyed It, and I didn't want to find out. But the rules of my incarceration bound me to this building, and this cat, and this ghoulish, empty part of town.

"Look, I can't rent you a truck," the claws dug in, "But I can maybe take our delivery truck out there, see if there's anything we want, do the deal there."

The claws retracted.

Campbell liked the idea—less risk on his part. We arranged a time to meet. As he passed beyond the stuffed bear into the real world, the Master's voice filled the room.

"You will take me with you."

"Of course, Master, of course." And I stroked that infernal cat's clammy skin with my cold fingers in the icebox of a showroom, and tried to remember what summer felt like.

THE VALLEY, STRETCHING OUT to the east for two hundred miles, glowed as if with pleasure as I drove the next morning. Spring in the high desert, the first I'd ever seen. The kind of beauty that breaks your heart, which is why the Master allowed the excursion: to remind me of the sun, so that I'd long for it every day inside the frigid pawn shop. As the sun rose proud through the March thunderheads, I resolved to savor every last moment I could squeeze out of the enterprise.

Tosetti's last house lived on an unremarkable street with an unremarkable name that stretched between 43rd and 44th on the west side of down, surrounded on all sides by perfectly respectable houses that had all started going to seed. An old neighborhood, filled with old people and houses dyed the color of children's laughter and flavored with the kinds of violence that only happen between loved ones. Campbell waited for me outside, sitting on the porch swing as if he'd been born there.

The stairs leading up to the house had once been painted in red lead-based oil to match the brick of the walkway from the street. Now, the faded brick-color peeled back in gashes to reveal the house's brittle flesh beneath, gray-white like the onion-skin of a venerable English grandmother.

In the topmost step, I found a brass plaque set flush with the porch decking. It read "Anthemum House, by Alan Tosetti." The lady had a name, and standing on her sitting-porch, I could feel her pain crawling up through my shoes. The Master could feel it too, and It paced Its disquiet from shoulder to shoulder across my leather traveling coat.

Campbell rose from his seat and approached the door, fumbling with his keys. After trying two different ones, wondering why they didn't work, and rifling through the rest of the set, he started patting his pockets.

"Is this your first time here?"

"No, I was here for inventory, but I just got the official keys yesterday. Usually I'd put them on my ring but...there." He drew a smaller ring out of a pocket concealed inside his flannel vest. "Last night I had an emergency at another property."

"How many more do you manage?"

"None. I do restoration. That's how they picked me for trustee of this place." The door clicked, he pushed it in. It opened directly onto the living room, crowded with pictures and nick-knacks and cruft two generations old. Dust stood proud of every surface, and tracks were visible on the hardwood where someone, presumably Campbell, had come through to review the place maybe a week ago.

Anthemum's arms were open to us. The Master leapt to the floor and lead the way into her secret places. Campbell followed, and I followed Campbell.

"That's some weird cat you've got," he said.

"Tell me about it."

He led me on a tour through the place, show-ing me this and that, admitting that he didn't know much about what might be interesting and what might not, and pointing out the little neon orange tabs on pieces that he intended to keep. We—or I, as Campbell put it—were free to take anything else. I was to move everything that looked interest-ing into the garage, and we'd dicker. What I didn't want, he'd probably burn in Anthemum's massive fireplace beneath the mantle where Tosetti—and his daughters—had died.

There was a lot to go through. Other people's memories, other people's joy, other people's passions. I did not see the Master for the next three days; It was busy on some urgent business with Anthemum. Maybe that was the real reason It had allowed me to do the survey.

I drove to and from in the evening, as I was obliged. I slept on my cot in the cold back office, and I ate my breakfast from the government surplus cans that came irregularly throughout the year. During the day, I drove out in the sunlight and returned in the moonlight, and each was like water for my withered heart.

And every day in Anthemum, I felt her warming. She had a terrible hunger, it echoed through every corridor. The doors hung always half open, like parched lips, no matter how I'd left them when last I used them. But the sense of tragedy that wafted through her like dust motes seemed to lighten with every item I removed to the garage. As if it stoked her eagerness to live again, perhaps even to live without killing those who came to visit her.

At least, that's what I thought at the time. Because I didn't understand what it was that, truly, she longed for.

Not until Tuesday.

I was sorting through the contents of a chest of drawers in her utility room, when I heard the Master's call. The short, insistent meow followed by the demonic whisper:

Come here, bondsman.

It didn't say where, but from the mewling I judged It had found Its way into the basement. I found It there, in the dim room smelling of creosote and old turpentine, curled up in Campbell's lap. Campbell sat at a card table in an old metal folding chair, checking some figures in white chalk on blue paper and glancing excitedly at the walls. I followed his gaze, and I could see why.

The basement walls had all been furred out, and all around, in irregular stacks half-buried in dirt and dust and cobwebs and boxes, were the unused materials. Dark stained oak beams, notched joinery, hardwood flooring planks, tubs of plaster, palates of lath. Campbell caught my eye and smiled.

"Look at this."

I did. It was a blueprint to finish the base-ment as a large entertaining space with French doors spilling the party-goers out into the back garden—yes, there were plans for finishing the garden as well.

"Looks like Tosetti's daughter didn't finish the place after all."

"Yeah." Campbell's skin was beading right in front of me. In his lap, the Master purred like a leopard claiming a tree. The Master only purred when It had made a deal to Its liking, and Its liking was often to nobody's advantage but Its own. "But look at this, LOOK at this!" He stabbed his feverish finger at the sketches. "It's all here. My God," he lifted his face to stare at the materials palates all around the musty basement. "It's all here."

"But surely you're only supposed to restore it to how he left it." The Master meowed and shifted unhappily on Campbell's lap. Its eyes narrowed at me, a voiceless warning. I decided to pretend I hadn't noticed. "If you finish it, it won't be Tosetti's house any longer, not in the historical-preservation sense."

The Master stood and walked across the table between us, then took Its customary place on my shoulders and began punishing me. The claws in the back of my neck were the least of it—the visions of my past sins, the reminders of the things I'd done and tried to do, the deaths I'd died attempt-ing to escape, all played over and over in my mind as my heart tightened, then blackened. Its voice whispered in the desolation: *You are mine. You will do as I say. Or you will suffer.* And then It underscored Its point, dredging up the kinds of memories that reduce the stoutest of men to tears, all while holding me rigid and not allowing me any expression. It trapped me inside, and then took control. I was Its marionette.

Campbell saw none of this. He appeared to be fighting with himself, struggling to avert a profound loss.

"But..." Campbell's face fell as my words sank in. I cheered behind my mask. I had a sickly intuition of the Master's plan—there was a cold, sadistic, predictable logic to the kinds of deals It made—but whether I was right or not, It could do nothing without Campbell's participation. And now It would use my body to undo the damage I'd done to Its plans. "I guess you're right. It's just..."

"It would be a fine thing to see it finished." My mouth made those comforting sounds, not I. Every time it moved, I felt sick. But I was locked away, separated from all communication to the world. All I had was the Master's unsympathetic ear.

"Yes," Campbell sighed, the fight going out of him, "Yes, it would be."

"You know," the Master said through me, as It moved my body around to stand beside him, "Tosetti employed workmen, even on this place. He only did the finishing touches himself."

"True." Campbell nodded, lifting himself cautiously, as if testing hopeful airspace to see if it was safe, "And...oh, but I don't have the budget for that."

My body shrugged. "You will when I pay you for the items in the garage."

"You think?"

My hand patted his back. "Let's find out. But first, show me what you'll do."

He took us on a tour of the basement, expostulating on the details of Tosetti's genius, the simple elegance that was destined to fill the unfinished space. Even as I nursed the awareness of the terrible price It would extract from him, I had to admit that seeing the house finished would be a fine thing.

Yes, the Master said to me, *you see it now.*

I wasn't sure I did. I did know I didn't want to.

Campbell led us through the brick-a-brack to the back. The French doors were covered with tacked-up plywood, but they opened well enough once he released the hook-catch. The grass in the back piled high with season after season of high wild grasses that had died and gone to seed without being eaten by wild goats—the fence was too high for them to leap—and the thick pad on the ground wafted rotting compost to my nose. I wanted to choke, but the Master was in control, and It kept me perfectly serene and encouraging as Campbell paced off the planters, the gazebo, the places for drought-tolerant fruit trees and flowers, the spots reserved for benches and lover's swings.

"Do you really think I could finish it?"

"That depends," said the Master, "On how good you are with a chisel. This place is your responsibility—do *you* think you can finish it?"

Campbell cast about carefully, as if weighing his vanity and desire against his good sense, and then, with a "Hell yes" he cast his fate to the wind.

"Excellent. Let's see if we can't finance you."

In the garage, the few dozen items I'd picked according to their value and saleability got their go-over by the Master in my skin. The Master had different criteria, and there were a few unremarkable items in the house that It excused my body to retrieve.

The Master's plans snapped into focus as I entered Anthemum again, this time without Campbell by my side. The first time I'd been in her without him. Stepping through the door, with the Master possessing me, I could hear her keening. The kind of desperate scream I'd once heard from my mother, while she held the broken body of our dog, run down in front of us by a pickup truck. The very air seemed to convulse in racking sobs of utter, inconsolable desolation. No new dawn would come, no end to grief, just the endless longing of a woman stuck on the knife-point of loss. Even accounting for the extra awareness the Master brought, this was a world apart from the wistful melancholy I felt when Campbell was present.

I should have seen it sooner. Thinking back over Anthamum's various residents, the pattern was clear. Single people lived here quite happily. Grief swallowed and smothered those already grieving. Families moved away. Lovers quickly died. She was monogamous, and desolate, and lonely—and very, very jealous.

There was no escaping the obvious:

The Master had already reached an arrangement, just not with Campbell.

In short order It selected a half-dozen perfectly ordinary things—a makeup compact, an old battered doll, an ordinary-looking leather satchel, and such-like—that might fetch a dime or a dollar at a garage sale, on a good day. It had designs for them, which, I knew, I'd become privy to the full horror of when the time came.

We made our way back to the garage and commenced with the dicker.

Campbell drove a hard bargain, or at least the Master wanted him to think so. They pressed back and forth over every item, arriving on a price that guaranteed that we'd be selling them at a slim loss, if they ever did move. But the Master didn't care about that—the antiques appealed to one section of clientele, the section that the Master was least interested in. The personal trinkets, ones that the house would never have let It take otherwise, those were Its true prize. Those, It paid for handsomely, with a line of credit guaranteeing that Anthemum would be finished to Tosetti's original specifications, and with one other, infinitely more valuable trade item.

You will not tell him, said the Master as It

released me. It didn't need an "or else." It hopped silently off my shoulders and padded away to see to Its own business. I was left to load the truck on my own.

Campbell helped, staging the heavier items for me, but never venturing out beyond the end of the driveway. He didn't intend to abandon me to the lifting at the other end, he just seemed to remember something urgent every time he got out that far. The deal was already in effect. Sooner or later he would figure out that he was bound to Anthemum, much as I was bound to the shop. A fellow prisoner, as yet blissfully unaware of his incarceration. Too excited about the project, too in love with Anthemum to realize he would never return home to his family, or that woman he wanted to marry.

I never knew love like that. I hope to God I never do.

I wanted to apologize. To explain to him that he was the price the Master paid for those trinkets. That Anthemum was a grief-shattered widow; she needed someone to make herself complete. And like a cuckold, she brooked no threat of intrusion on her affections. Whether driven by the ghost of Tosetti to find completion, or driven by grief at his loss to find love again, the empty house needed an empty man. And it had found one.

When the Master returned, we climbed into the truck, thunked it into gear, and set off home.

The shop was cold. The fire raged in the hearth like a false promise. Part of my lot. Part of the deal. The shop was mine, until I paid off my debt. Until someone else got into hock further than they could pay it off. I had to tend it in the cold, and smile at the customers, and listen to the stories of the things they bought.

And in the lonely hours, I hear the Master's voice, telling the stories behind every trinket, every treasure, every collected soul.

It's the interest on the loan.

Sunday Morning Giraffe

IT WAS 3 AM ON a Sunday, in December, and Aldo wanted a giraffe. If Aldo had lived in Kenya, this wouldn't have been a problem. A broken-down gambling boomtown on the edge of nowhere in the high desert of Nevada, though, was less conducive to giant browsers.

If Aldo didn't get a giraffe, he wouldn't sleep. And it *couldn't* be a toy giraffe either—it had to be a proper, three-stories tall African savanna cow with an ultra long neck and brown spots. It might be enough to get him in close proximity with a giraffe, convince him that it was his, but housed at the zoo for safe-keeping.

Too bad the zoo was closed for the winter.

But if Aldo didn't get his giraffe, nobody else in the house would get any sleep either, and they knew it. He'd scream, and cry, and wander the house all night in his slipper-foot PJs picking up knick-nacks and shaking them, as if he could evoke their inner giraffe-ness. That's what he'd done before when he wanted a submarine, and the time before that when he wanted a dinosaur.

His parents, Bob and Judy, weren't given to indulging him. When his strange requests started—it was water balloons at Thanksgiving—they told him not to be silly. They were proof against his preschool manipulation techniques. His mother, particularly, was 85 proof gin against his manipulation techniques, while his father's resolve was borne of a successful military career, from which he retired with a full pension. They'd become parents late in life, after raising an orphaned niece and nephew had hardened them against childish desires. If the boy was unreasonable he deserved to meet with frustration. Water balloons at the Thanksgiving dinner table were absolutely unreasonable.

They'd put their foot down. There would be no water balloons.

Bob's boss was over for dinner that day, and he'd worn a very formal, and very old, serge suit. A suit so old that it wasn't fireproof. When passing the mashed potatoes, he'd lingered too long over the silver candelabra that Judy had set out as a centerpiece. The poor man went up like a torch. By the time they put him out, he had burns over his whole left side and had to be rushed to the hospital, but that was nothing to the steel-eyed anger in five-year-old Aldo's eyes when the paramedics left.

"What's wrong, Aldo?" Judy had asked.

"I said I wanted water balloons. You wouldn't listen. You never listen." Then he stormed out, and they didn't see him again for several hours. After the afternoon's excitement, they didn't bother to follow him—they had other kinds of fretting to do.

It wasn't until the incident with the submarine that they learned to indulge him when they could. He'd come in to his father's study one Saturday night, insisting that he wanted a submarine. The next day, terrorists bombed the reservoir dam.

At that point, they got the idea: when Aldo wanted something totally inappropriate, they'd better listen. They didn't know how he knew—they were very sure that he was too young to understand.

So, at three in the morning on a Sunday, when Aldo woke up his parents clutching his teddy bear, pulling at its ears, and demanding a giraffe in that half-absent way, Bob rolled out of bed and tried to find his pants without mooning his son. They drove immediately to the zoo, even though it was closed. On the road, Bob tried to pry details out of the boy, but all Aldo would say was "It is the will of Almighty Flarn."

Flarn. The rodent deity on the boy's favorite cartoon, some claptrap with talking barn animals. Bob gave up his probing.

The overcast which hung low in the winter lit the night red with reflected light from the city's preferred industry. The zoo's entrance, out on the north edge of town, was overgrown with long-dead ivy. The wan sodium streetlights did it no favors, splattering it with the color of bile, making skeleton-finger shadows grow from the tangle on the ancient brick walls and wrought-iron gates.

Wrought-iron, chained against entry. Bob coaxed Aldo up onto his back and hiked around the side, looking for some kind of service entrance. Maybe they wouldn't be worried about security this time of year—the only thing on this end of town in the winter were the snow plows. And the wolves.

Around the back they found a loading dock, and a garbage truck, and a custodian doing his late-night rounds with earphones on. Not hard to sneak past for a former infantry officer. Inside, Bob took his son to the tallest of the big barns in which, judging by the smell, the animals sheltered for the winter.

And in the tallest, there were three giraffes—two adults, tall as trees, and a juvenile. Bob let Aldo down, and the boy pranced up to the tall chain-link fence that cordoned off the entryway from the pen.

"There you go, Aldo," Bob said, "three giraffes."

Aldo held the fence like a spider monkey. He didn't respond to his father's voice, but after a moment his hands came off the fence and his arms folded over his chest. He turned around, stamping the ground with great purpose.

"I said I want a giraffe."

"Aldo, those are giraffes."

"I want a real giraffe!"

"Those *are* real giraffes." And so it went, round and round, until Bob gave up and took Aldo around to all the other barns that weren't locked. Maybe Aldo meant an elephant? A hippo? A parrot?

No such luck. He meant a giraffe, alright. But he seemed to think that *real* giraffes were smaller, and nothing Bob could say would make a difference. "Real" meant whatever Aldo said it meant, and Bob was already frightened enough of the boy that his pride kept well out of the way.

And so an early morning excursion in the name of getting the kid to shut up and go back to bed turned into an all day journey. First, they got caught by the custodian and kicked out of the zoo. Then, they visited animal shelters. Then, they visited pet shops. Nothing remotely fitting Aldo's personal definition of "giraffe" came to hand.

Parents were stupid. Pretty much all adults were stupid, but parents especially. Okay, sure, they could read thicker books than he could, but only because they made him turn his lights off at nine o'clock and he sometimes lost the bookmark and had to start over. They didn't listen to him, either, no matter how clear he made himself, because they thought *he* was stupid.

At least they were listening a little bit now. Good thing, because according to the word of Almighty Flarn, without a giraffe everything would be ruined. It had to be a particular kind of giraffe, too. Aldo knew that for sure. It couldn't be an imaginary giraffe or a stuffed giraffe, it had to be as real as Legos. But it couldn't be one of those mooking big ones, the ones from the zoo as tall as a building. How did his father think he'd fit *that* in his room?

He could see it in his head, but finding words that his stupid parents would understand was driving him bonkers, even though his dad got him ice cream for lunch. If he saw the inside of one more pet store or toy store he was going to throw a fit, just to teach the old man to listen. Or maybe he'd just shut up and say he didn't want it anymore, and let them find out what happened when they didn't listen. That would teach them but good.

THEY WERE STARTING TO get into parts of town where Bob wasn't comfortable bringing a child. Truth to tell, he wouldn't want to be here on his own, either. Not at his age. He sold life insurance and knew the kind of surcharge they slapped on people who lived south of 50th street. But short of going to the circus in the casino, the place down here was the last place to look.

It was a pawn shop on the edge of the old suburbs, where nobody lived since they did the bomb tests out in the desert when Bob was a boy. Radiation. Only the moron who owned the shop was crazy enough to stay out here.

Bob hadn't heard of the place until the last two pet shops on 45th. The sales girls at both places had told him about it after Aldo started pitching fits. They seemed to take pity—either on the boy, or on him. They both mentioned the pawn shop, saying "If it exists, that guy will have it. He's creepy, though." Or words to that effect.

If they hadn't said, that, Bob would have gotten the idea the moment he walked through the door and found himself face-to-face with a stuffed, ravening wolverine. He jumped, which made little Aldo roll his eyes and growl. He and Judy were going to have to do something about that boy—these premonitions of his had given him entirely too high an idea of himself. Any self-respecting parent would have given the brat a thorough thrashing. Bob hadn't, and he kicked himself every day for it.

Aldo, meanwhile, had had enough of Bob standing around looking at the wolverine, and scurried past.

"Aldo!" Goddamn kid wouldn't listen. He just ran on in.

Bob entered with more caution, and then wished he hadn't come down. The place was ice cold—even though a fire burned brightly in the hearth—and festooned with skulls and occult artifacts of the sort that he used to hear about in high school. The kind the kids that dressed in black always wore around their necks. This was probably the kind of place where they sold contracts with the devil.

Aldo was drawn right away to the display case, full of trinkets and collectibles. His little face pressed up against the glass as if there were puppies on the other side. "That's it! That's it! Daddy! That's it!"

The object of Aldo's adulation was real, all right, and it was a giraffe, but Bob couldn't figure out how it qualified as a real giraffe. Bob shrugged and rang the bell on the counter.

As if summoned from the pit of hell, a sharp-dressed young man wearing a single glove appeared. An old, diseased-looking cat rode on his shoulders. At Bob's request, he produced the trinket from the showcase.

"Here we go," he said in a gentle drawl, "genuine nineteen thirty-six giraffe pull-toy made by Lambert And Sons. Gorgeous condition."

Pawnbrokers evidently had the same definition of "gorgeous" as used car dealers. The toy, eighteen inches tall, was scratched and beat up like it had been well used and then left to rot in a forgotten attic for sixty or seventy years. It's left eye was missing, its left ear bent double and rusted on the exposed metal. The colors had faded from brown and white to a kind of dull purpleish over equally dull yellow, and its cast iron wheels were rusted solid in place.

The pawnbroker wanted three hundred bucks. Bob tried to dicker, but at the first suggestion that he might be willing to pass up the giraffe, Aldo lost it. He ran in place and wailed loud enough to wake the dead—in this shop, Bob fully expected the dead to start shambling in and asking if they could hock their gold teeth.

"Okay okay okay, shut up," he muttered, and dug into his pocket for a credit card. "Fine, I'll take it."

The proprietor looked at the little shit, then up at Bob, something approaching pity in his cold, dead eyes. "I'll tell you what, cause you've had a bad day, I'll take the kid off your hands."

"What?" Bob reflexively pulled Aldo to him, but the offer wasn't without its appeal.

The proprietor chuckled. It made the hairs on Bob's neck crawl. "Just kidding. I'll do a hundred fifty for you. Make your day a little better."

"Oh." Bob sighed with less relief than he really felt. "Okay."

Ten minutes later, they left the shop with Aldo's prize. All the boy's peevishness was gone. He pranced and danced and held the ridiculous piece of trash up like it was the most beautiful prize a boy could ever get.

"ALMIGHTY FLARN!" ALDO LAID down at the baseboard between his bed and the wall and whispered as loud as he dared. His parents were watching TV and having one of their "whatever shall we do about the boy" talks. Aldo had overheard a lot of them, and they were always nasty. They talked about things like boarding school, and reform school, and teaching him proper discipline, and taking away his books. So far, it hadn't come to anything, but one of these days they'd figure out how to get rid of him.

At least, they *thought* so.

"Almighty Flarn!" he said, "I got it!"

A series of little scratches came from behind the wall. They skittered along from the closet, along the baseboard, and around the corner to behind Aldo's nightstand.

Good boy, came the small, but powerful, voice from behind the nightstand, *I knew I could count on you.*

"You wanna see it?" Aldo reached up on his bed and seized the toy, brought it back down to show it to Flarn the Almighty. "I've got it right here. Don't worry, they're watching TV."

Tentatively, a little pink nose poked out from beneath the bedside bureau. The whiskers on the end twitched as if to make sure everything was clear. Then, the head of a large, tan rat poked out and looked around suspiciously. Once it was satisfied that nothing dangerous lurked nearby, it scampered the rest of the way out and ran up the giraffe.

You have done well, my boy, the rat said. *This is the very thing.*

Aldo smiled as big as his face would let him. Almighty Flarn was a wise old rat—he'd been giving Aldo secret missions for months now. Important things, for which he'd be richly rewarded. Almighty Flarn had promised that one day, there would be no more lights out time, and his parents would stop getting in his way, and he could read all night if he wanted to.

In fact, the kindly rat had promised he'd be getting his reward soon, after this mission was done.

"So?"

The rat seemed startled, and twitched its whiskers at him. *Yes, young Aldo?*

"When do I get my prize?"

All in good time, my boy.

Aldo crossed his arms and glared. "You promised!"

Yes, I promised. But this giraffe is the first step of your reward. The rest will become clear soon—maybe by Saturday, if we are very lucky.

Aldo chewed his lip cynically. Almighty Flarn hadn't steered him wrong yet, but sometimes adults used delays as a way to weasel out of their promises. But Flarn was a rat, not a weasel, so it might be okay. "Okay," he said, "Saturday. I'll wait till then, but you better come through, or I won't help you anymore."

You are most fair, my friend. I shall endeavor to deliver by Saturday.

Aldo picked the rat up and pet him, then set him on his shoulder and crawled into bed. It had been a long day hunting giraffes, and he didn't have to read more than a paragraph or two before he fell asleep.

* * *

TWO DAYS LATER, WHILE Aldo read in the living room, his parents reset the traps to deal with their rat infestation and talked again about getting a cat. Judy didn't want one—Aldo wouldn't know how to behave around it, and he'd mess up the house when he changed the litter box. Bob, however, was sick of the whole rigmarole and insisted. They'd get one this weekend, come hell or high water, and Aldo could just suck it up. About time the boy learned some proper discipline anyway—Judy would just have to learn to be firm with him.

Aldo could hear the whole conversation. He shook with anger when they started arguing about whether to start him at a boarding school come the spring semester.

ON THE EAST END of town, however, events unfolded that would bear directly on their decision, and on Flarn's promises:

That evening, a certain man was getting out of jail.

An emaciated, wiry slip of a man, he was getting out on a normal good-behavior release for a felony burglary; a four year sentence reduced to eight months. At about four in the afternoon, he was hustled out the front gate with the clothes on his back and a wallet containing twenty dollars for bus fare in his pocket, in case his wife was working when he was released.

She wasn't, though. Cynthia London was waiting in her denim jacket and threadbare jeans, leaning against his jalopy Camaro with a shit-eating grin on her face. When her man got out of the gate, she lit two cigarettes and held one out for him.

He saw her and plodded across the lot, looking years older than when he'd gone in.

It wasn't a sweet reunion. He didn't want to talk about his time inside, and he got angry whenever she tried to talk about her life in the months he'd been gone. He'd served his time, and wanted to forget it. But once they were out of sight of the jail, his posture relaxed and a bit of a smile returned to his face.

A couple miles on, they pulled off onto a dirt road and screwed on the hood of the car—the best sex either of them had had since before he was arrested. Mark had only had the guys in the shower, and he didn't like any of them, or what they did to him, or how the prison guards seemed not to care except the one time when, fighting him off, he'd gotten his jaw broken. Cynthia had the landlord, because with Mark in jail they didn't make enough to pay rent on their shitty little apartment, and she didn't even want to think about him, let alone admit it to Mark. Besides, now that Mark was out, they could get a new place.

After they were done, and had good smiles all around, Mark asked the big question:

"You got the ticket?"

Cynthia pulled a yellowing pawn check out of her jacket pocket and held it up. He took it from her, and she bounced in place and squealed. "Oh, baby, we're gonna be rich!"

He caught her up and gave her another good,

solid kiss, then smacked her ass and sent her to the passenger side.

They got lunch on the way at a casino—the first honest-to-god steak that Mark had tasted in over eight months. A couple hours later, though, when they reached the rickety pawn shop on the edge of no-man's-land, the smiles disappeared.

"You see, sir," the proprietor said, "You didn't collect your valuables in the time allotted. We put them out on sale two months ago. If you'll read the back of your ticket..."

"Now look here," Mark said, "I don't give a flying fuck about the ticket. I need that toy! Who bought it? When?"

"I'm sorry, sir, that information is private."

"Is it now? We'll just have to see about that."

Mark had learned a few things about persuasion in prison. Cynthia could see that. But if he didn't get the info, Mark's ire would turn on her, and she didn't fancy a beating the first day he was out of the big house. She wanted her goddamn honeymoon.

She thought something like this might happen—and, truth to tell, she didn't have the money to buy the toy back anyway—so she'd brought along their little revolver. She pulled it out of her purse and shot it at the floor.

"Now," she said, "I'm thinkin' you're gonna give us that there address."

He didn't take a lot more persuading, but she smashed his nose with the gun afterward anyway.

Mark needed to know she was still on his side, no matter what. Yeah, the guy might call the cops, but they'd be long gone by then. They wrapped him up in duct tape and took off for the swanky high-rent suburbs, where everyone had their own yard.

* * *

ALDO WAS READING. IT was after nine, but he'd stolen his dad's flashlight and snuck it under the covers. He used the extra thick blanket in the winter, and he was sure nobody would be able to see the light underneath.

Almighty Flarn sat on his shoulder while Aldo read aloud, whispering out the story of *Treasure Island* from his enormous illustrated edition.

"See, that's Long John Silver there, with the peg leg. This parrot here on his shoulder is Cap'n Flint," he pointed at the illustration, then flipped the page and started reading the narration again.

"Aldo!" his mother called. "I can hear you reading in there!" Her footsteps stalked down the hardwood hallway and he heard the door open. Almighty Flarn dashed into hiding. Aldo didn't see where—he was too busy trying to douse the light quick as he could, but his hand slipped on the button. The covers wooshed away over his head.

His mother towered over him, vexed and red-faced as a damn dirty pirate. Aldo froze. She didn't get that mad very often. "I've told you not to read after nine. You," she snatched the book and the light from him, "are in big trouble. Your father's right, you need discipline. You're going to that boarding school next term, so help me God."

"I am not! I'm not going to any damn school and you can't make me!"

She smacked him across the face. "Language! Oh, Aldo, you've done it now. There's nothing more I can do to protect you. Not one thing. I'm going to send your father in here and..."

Something in the front of the house crashed. Aldo heard his father yelling, and a woman screaming. His mother forgot all about him and dashed out the bedroom door, taking his book with her.

Aldo, frozen in shock, tried to fight back tears. If they saw him cry, he was a goner. They'd send him off for sure. Then how would he talk to Almighty Flarn?

The row in the front room was getting louder. People were using words he'd only heard late at night when he snuck out of bed to the balcony, when his father was watching war movies.

Aldo, came the small whisper from under his pillow, *it's time. Put the giraffe on the night stand and hide under the bed.*

"But...but..."

Quickly, my boy. Your reward is here!

Aldo snapped to. He grabbed the giraffe from his toy shelf. A heavy thing, what with being made of metal and all. He set it on the night stand and dove under the bed. Almighty Flarn joined him. He pet the rat because it made him feel better, and the Almighty whispered reassurances:

They won't hurt you, young friend. I promise. My people will be free, and you will be free, and the world will be as it should once again.

In another part of the house, Aldo heard gunshots. The noise started him crying again, and he clutched Almighty Flarn to his chest. There were one, two, then silence. Then, nobody was yelling anymore. A second later, he heard two more bangs. Then, the shouting started again, and he heard footfalls rushing through the house, and crashing noises like someone was knocking things off shelves. Then more shouting. More bad words.

Then, someone came into his room. His heart thumped so hard in his ears that he was sure whoever-it-was could hear it. He held his breath. The steps stopped just inside the door, then a woman's voice shouted "Mark! Mark! I found it!"

The woman's feet ran around his bed to the night stand. He heard her lift up the giraffe and toss it onto the bed. He heard squeaking and rattling noises, and then heavier footsteps. Mark (Aldo guessed) tramped into the room.

"You got it?"

More rattling. Then:

"Woo! We got it baby! Fifty thousand fucking dollars!"

Almighty Flarn whispered *They found the*

diamonds. You're safe now. They won't harm you.

"Are you sure?" Aldo whispered as quiet as he could, but on the bed above he heard the man say:

"Wait. What the fuck was that?"

A second later, the end of a gun raised the bedskirt and an ugly, leathery face peeked under the bed. "Well, what do we have here?" The man—Mark—chuckled. "You just come on outta there, boy."

Aldo nodded. He stuffed Almighty Flarn down his shirt and scooted backwards until he was out from under the bed. The woman laid a hand on him, as if she wanted to protect him.

Across the bed, Mark stood up and fingered the gun. He looked to the woman, then down to Aldo, then stamped the ground and stalked in a circle. "Sheeit, what're we gonna do now?"

"You wouldn't tell no one," the woman said, "Would you, darlin'?"

"Um...uh..." Aldo didn't know what to say. But he heard Flarn's small voice whispering from inside his pajamas.

Say it depends.

"It depends."

"Depends huh?" Mark said. "Depends on what?"

Taking his cue from Almighty Flarn, Aldo said "Depends on if I can read until midnight."

"Say that again, son?"

"Mom and dad are poop heads. They won't let me read when I get in bed. Will you?" Aldo wasn't sure about this, but he repeated Flarn's words. He trusted Flarn. Flarn had never steered him wrong.

He looked up at the woman. She was smiling—a kind sort of smile, too. Not the strained tolerance his own mother always smiled with. She looked over at Mark, who looked like he was about to have the fall-aparts.

She patted him on the shoulder. "You stay here a moment, darlin'. I gotta talk to my man." She walked around the bed and pulled Mark aside, but they talked loud enough for him to hear if he concentrated.

"Come on, baby, he's a good kid, and we can't have none of our own. We always wanted a smart boy like that—he'd grow up and help out, you know he would. Keep us right when we get old. Give us grandbabies maybe."

"I...I don't know. They'd find us."

"Not if he was in with us. He wouldn't run—he doesn't like it here. Come on, honey, for me?"

"Well..." Mark scratched the gun barrel against his forehead, then winced. "Goddamn it. Ah, fucking burns! Shit. Okay, I can't kill no kid. I say we take and dump him at the Salvation Army."

"No, no, no, honey. Take a good look at him. He'll be a good boy."

Mark looked at Aldo. Aldo looked down at the bed, not sure what to do.

"You'll be a good boy, won't you honey?" the woman said. "Go on a trip with us? See the world?"

"Well..."

Say yes, Aldo. This is your reward. This is what I promised you.

"Well..."

Go on, Aldo. I'll come with you. I'll make sure they let you read as long as you want.

"Well, you promise you'll let me read till midnight?"

"We can't have you keeping us up, darlin'."

"I'll read under the covers. It won't be any problem. But you'll let me read? And get me books when I run out?"

"Any books you want, honey. I promise."

Aldo looked up at Mark. The man's eyes were wide, almost crossed, like he'd just seen a dog with a bird's head. "Mark? You'll let me read too?"

"Uh...sure. I'll let you read. But you can't tell nobody about us, or how you got hooked up with us. You tell people you're our son, and you be a good boy."

Aldo brightened. "I'll be good, I promise! I can bring my rat?" Then he whispered to Almighty Flarn "You'll come with me, like you promised?"

"Rat?" The woman looked vaguely horrified.

"Yeah." He pulled Flarn out of his shirt and set him up on his shoulder. "He's no trouble. He just likes to sit on my shoulder when I read. He likes lettuce and crackers."

"Yeah, fine, whatever," Mark said. "What's your name, boy?"

"Aldo."

"Okay, Aldo, you're gonna need a new name. What you want we should call you when we're out on the road?"

Aldo didn't have to think twice. "Call me Jim." The guy reminded him a bit of Long John Silver.

"Alright Jim. This here's Cynthia, and she's your new momma. You mind her and me, and we won't have no trouble. Now you pack some clothes in a bag, and get your book, and we'll be on our way."

ALDO PACKED HIS BAG, Almighty Flarn at his ear, telling him what to bring. He had to get his book from his mother—she was still clinging to it, trying to keep it from him, even though she was laying dead as a dirty sea dog in the foyer. They set off into the night, and Aldo hunkered down in the back seat with a blanket, and his flashlight, and his book, and Almighty Flarn, who was as true as his word.

And he got to read as long as he wanted. And nobody said anything different.

CHICKEN NOODLE GRAVITY

I HATE TO START OUT this way, but before we get to the reason I'm standing on this stool with a fez on my head, in the middle of the night, in front of a double-cal-king bed in a furniture store—which, yes, Officer, I swear I'll confess I broke into illegally—before we get to any of that, there's something I have to tell you. I know it's awful, evil, and just plain wrong, but there's no way around it, and you won't understand anything else unless I say this right up front, so here goes:

Stephen was stoned.

And when I say "stoned" I mean he'd eaten enough brownies and smoked enough pot to put the economies of five or six minor countries into a severe, long-term deficit crisis.

It was okay, though. I didn't mind. It helped him cope with the chemo. Mellowed him out. We didn't have to fight over who got to hold the remote. He was better in bed too—not as neurotic. Didn't complain about my mustache when I kissed him. Suits me right for shacking up with a clean freak.

The weed was my revenge—well, the fact that the weed made it possible for him to eat. We had to grow our own—only way we could afford it, though I swear we probably spent as much on the electricity as we would have on the bud. Not a great climate for it, not in the winter.

So, the revenge part—that would be his appetite. When he smoked, it came back. It was the only time it came back. And there were only two things he could handle:

Brownies.

And chicken noodle soup. The really rancid stuff that came in a red and white can.

I swear, by all that's good and holy and a bowl of Ex-Lax besides, that was all he could eat. And he hated chocolate almost as much as he hated the soup. Feeding him the soup and brownies was my revenge on him for getting sick in the first place.

Not that I blamed him about the soup. A hundred forty years after it was invented, that stuff still smells like salted famine and disease glopping out of the can.

But after Stephen lost all his hair, for the third time, I got to love that smell. Not because it smelled any better, but because every time I smelled it I knew he'd be around at least long enough to eat it. Sometimes, a little bit of hope is all you need to keep going. When your life is filled with words like "pancreatic," "stage four," and "terminal," you learn to live with what you can get.

So we smoked like chimneys, screwed like carpenters, sang like sailors, and gambled like day-traders. I didn't give much of a damn that the money wouldn't last much longer than him.

But he just. Kept. Lasting. He didn't want to let me go any more than I wanted to let him go.

First it was the money. Then it was the house. Then it was the car. But it didn't matter. As long as I could keep growing the green, and opening those red and white cans.

It went on like that all winter.

When they diagnosed him, they said he'd last five weeks. We'd made it five months, and we weren't going to make it much longer without changing *something*—and whatever it was, we were going to have to get creative.

I was still employed. My job at the casino paid enough in tips that we should have been okay, and my insurance covered all his doctor visits. But the meds killed us. Cancer drugs move so fast that the difference in survival comes down to what month you're diagnosed, now. That small-cell lung cancer you've got today will kill you, but the tumor your brother discovers in six weeks will be treatable, and the one your mom gets a month after that will be curable.

If you can stay alive long enough, then you can stay alive period. That's the deal. And that's why every penny I earned in salary and tips went to his drugs, and it's why I ate that revolting chicken noodle soup night after night while we smoked up and watched old episodes of *Doctor Who.*

When I say we spent every penny on the drugs, I'm not kidding. I walked to work. Some weeks, I did the laundry by hand because we couldn't afford the electricity to wash our socks. But we had to eat, and my salary meant we were too rich for the food bank.

I had one option left. A last chance. I'd been selling off my old comic books to keep us in soup and vitamins, and myself in vegetables so I could stay healthy enough to take care of him. But I didn't have a lot that was valuable—stuff that's been well-loved doesn't resell well to collectors. With only a handful left, I needed a way to unload them in a place that might give me a little cash for them.

Marks—casino customers, you understand—always need a fresh source of dough, and when they have a few drinks in them, they get to talking. Over the years, I heard them talking, over and over, about this one pawn shop down past third street that paid high rates. Creepy place, they said, out where nobody in their right mind worked. Out where the city finally gave up and admitted it had turned into suburbs. Right on the edge of the hot zone.

Two miles out past the end of the bus line. Long walk with a box of old comics, but at least it wasn't raining.

I got there at four forty-five, just before closing. The broken-down gray bungalow had front windows stuffed to bursting with knick-knacks. The front entry was nearly blocked with large stuffed predators.

And it was cold. Outside, the desert's spring dusk shone orange and warm, but inside, even with the fire roaring in the hearth, my breath billowed in front of my face.

I dropped the box on the glass display case, above the crosses, the pentacles, the talismans from a dozen different religions. I rang the service bell sitting next to the brass idol of Siva.

One thing you can give the guy that ran this place: He could collect like no pack rat I'd ever known.

"May I help you, sir?"

A young guy, maybe twenty. Short black hair, nice broad shoulders. Cute as a button, except for the hollow eyes. And the creepy, hairless cat perched on his shoulders like Long John Silver's parrot.

Okay, so I liked *Treasure Island* as a kid. I thought Long John was hot. Get over it.

"Do you buy comics?"

He nodded.

"How much for these?" I shoved the box at him. He pulled the yellowed strapping tape back, opened up the lid on my last bit of treasure.

He pulled them out, one by one, smiling over each, laying them on the counter like they were made of lace. At least, maybe, they'd be going to a good home.

It made parting with the last piece of my childhood a bit easier.

The cat walked down his arm and seemed to pore over them as well.

"Yeah, oh, yes, these are nice ones," said the shopkeeper, "you know a lot of these are older than me?"

I chuckled. "I wouldn't be surprised."

"So, how much are you looking for?" Like a real pawnbroker—always let the customer open the bid.

My stomach rumbled. I hoped Stephen hadn't lit up yet, or he'd be starving.

"Honestly? Anything I can get."

He clucked his tongue at me. I winced. I started in a bad bargaining position, and I had nowhere to go but down. Time to grovel.

"I've got...I need to get food money. My husband is sick...dying. All our money's going to the treatment. We're out of things to eat. This..." I put my hands down on the spread of memories, "is all I have left."

He sighed, like he was gearing up to insult my mother. "Well, I gotta tell you, it's not worth much. These are great old issues, but there's nothing top drawer here..."

"I liked off-kilter stuff when I was a kid."

"And you liked it a lot. Rare is good, but collectors want 'em mint. These...these I can't move. I'd be buying decorations and as you can see," he nodded around the frigid room, hung heavy with all manner of gaudy memorabilia, "I don't need any more. I could give you maybe...ten bucks?"

I nodded. I could feel my shoulders, maybe for the first time in my life, fall a little bit. Up until that moment, I don't think I'd ever felt beaten. A year before, we'd had everything, and nowhere to go but on and up. Now, the last piece of my life that wasn't already dying was worth the price of two meals. That's all. Just enough soup for two more nights together.

"Forget it." I ran my hand under the flimsy little books, pushing them back into a modest, almost non-existent pile. "It was a mistake coming here. I'm sorry I wasted your time, I just...I'm sorry."

I put them in the box and made to pick it up, but he put his hand on it. "Hold on a minute. Like I said, they're good books. What would you say to a trade?"

"What kind of trade?"

"Follow me."

He beckoned me toward the back. Lacking anything better to do, I followed him.

The store room behind was as crowded as the display room out front, and seemed to stretch back forever. Filing racks stuttering away from me like giant dominoes poised to fall with the slightest push.

He led me about halfway down, then swept his arm down an aisle. "Back here."

On the floor, a pack of maybe twenty of those damned little red and white cans. I had to grab the shelves to steady myself.

"I get these in here every so often, they send them out from the lab—they order more than they can use. Some of the stuff I sell on, some of it I hand off to the food bank. No reason I can't hand it off to you. There isn't a lot, but..."

SO THERE IT WAS. Twenty-four cans—twenty-three little ones on wrapped flat with one missing, and one family sized. I'd save that one for next time I had two days off in a row, so we could grab lunch and dinner out of it.

That night, for dinner, I opened two of the cans and poured them into the saucepan. While it heated, I checked over the label. They were government cans, standard condensed-soup paint job notwithstanding. *Singularity Soup: The Singular Experience.*

Cute.

At least the ingredients list was the same as yesterday's soup can, which meant Stephen would be able to keep it down. I passed him a joint, and put the Ninth Doctor on TV, and waited for it to boil.

For six glorious nights, we had each other. I turned cards in the day, and at night I turned him over in our bed and grabbed every spare touch I could manage without wearing him out too much.

SATURDAY, HALFWAY THROUGH OUR new lease on life—six more days of soup, maybe seven if I stretched it, until I had to find food again, somehow. But I knew I wouldn't need to. Stephen still kept his food down, but his skin was going sallow, and he had trouble now making it into the bathroom without help. I couldn't help him much longer.

He wouldn't last until the soup ran out. I got the sneaking suspicion he was holding on long enough to see the tenth doctor.

That would be tomorrow.

Well, if that was the time we had, then it was what we had.

I took the family-sized can from the pantry and squeezed the can opener onto the lip, but instead of the familiar hiss of air rushing into the vacuum-sealed steel, I heard a distant clang—like someone had knocked a tool off a shelf in the garage, except we didn't have a garage anymore. Just the studio apartment in the low-rent district.

Odd.

But Stephen didn't seem to notice. He was sleeping on our bed.

Lifted the can and looked at it, but the weight felt right. Maybe a bit on the heavy side, but not much.

I shook it. Felt like soup to me.

So I set it back down on the counter and cranked the can-opener handle.

As I progressed around the lip, the serrated edge of the lid started to curl in, like something was pulling it.

But it wasn't until the can opener was halfway around that I began to think that something was really, *really* wrong with this can.

The middle of the lid dimpled in—just a little—and made an adorable blooping sound, like a kid with a noisemaker.

I stopped. Looked at the pit. It stretched, slowly, down into the can—and the further it plunged the faster it went, until the entire edge tore free at once and dropped into the...

Light?

Light. A kind I'd never seen before.

And wind. As if the can were trying to suck the whole room in.

"Bill? Bill? What the hell is going on in there?" Stephen's voice, thin as onionskin, as alarmed as it could sound without breaking.

"Nothing," I fumbled around in the Tupperware drawer, found a plastic lid, "Nothing, I just bumped the hood fan. I...shit...sorry, didn't mean to wake you up." I slammed the lid on the can, and all the light and wind stopped at once. "How are you feeling?"

"Ask a different question."

I shrugged. Pretty fair, as demands went. "You want fries with your soup?"

"God, if I could..." He chuckled. A good sound.

We had to eat, and whatever was in the big can, it wasn't soup. I cracked open a couple of the little ones and poured 'em into the saucepan, turned on the gas.

Between preparing the tray tables with the bowls and spoons ready for ladling in front of the TV, and waiting for the dinner to boil, I chanced to pick up the can with the portable storm inside.

The other cans—the smaller ones, you understand—all had their labels painted on. This one had a printed paper label.

The ingredients list was the same. It had the same *Singularity Soup* legend across the top, but underneath, where the others said simply *Condensed Chicken Noodle* this one instead read *Chicken Noodle: Ultra Condensed*.

As to the difference between *Condensed* and *Ultra-Condensed*? I hadn't a clue.

I didn't have time to investigate further. The smell of skunkweed and chicken stock choked the house, and the liquid in the pan broke into a rolling boil.

DINNER AND THE GOOD Doctor. Two episodes tonight, not just one.

We'd met at a party where they were showing old Tom Baker episodes—two gay Americans who both grew up secretly obsessing over a suave, asexual, time traveling Brit.

It occurred to me that night, as I watched him sleep on our bed in front of the TV, that I might have quit my job months ago and taken every moment with him. I'd have had more minutes, and he'd have had a quicker death. Kinder. We'd have had the money to treat him for a couple months, maybe, before resorting to the secret stash of heroin I'd managed to obtain from the pusher at work.

Totaling up the minutes, we'd have had more together. The problem was, though, that the sooner he died, the more minutes I'd have to live after he'd gone. There were already too many to count. I didn't want to add to them. So I kept him alive as long as I could, for my own sake. Because I couldn't let him go.

Because I was a selfish fuck, and I knew it.

But he seemed to understand. He didn't want to leave either. So he never objected. Even when the pain and the humiliation were worst, during the chemo sessions, he never asked me for that injection, even though he knew I wouldn't be able to refuse him.

I COULDN'T SLEEP. I didn't have anywhere to be tomorrow anyway. There wasn't any alcohol in the house to numb the impending loss—even if there was, I'm not sure I'd have taken any. Didn't seem dignified, somehow. But I couldn't focus enough to read, and I didn't want to put anything on the box that might wake Stephen, cheat him out of his rest.

Eventually I found myself in the kitchenette, studying that can. With the lid on it behaved, once again, like an ordinary soup can. Just a little heavier than normal. It moved like it was full of liquid with maybe a little air space inside for sloshing.

But I'd opened it. I knew it wasn't soup inside.

For the sheer hell of it, I took a knife and cut the label off. It was an ordinary paper label, like any other. Underneath, the can was smooth and shiny—which was a bit odd. A normal soup can is ribbed.

I risked a peek under the lid. The minute I cracked it open, the wind started, as if it wanted to suck all the air into the can. Good thing I had a healthy grip—it almost tore the lid out of my hand and pulled it down into the light in the center.

A light as sharp in the night's half-light as if I'd poked a knitting needle into my eye.

I slammed the lid down again. What the hell was it?

The wind was suction, no doubt about it. And whatever was in there was sucking everything into it, so long as there was any window to the outside world.

But what could do that?

I looked at the label again. *Ultra-Condensed.*

On impulse I looked at the nutrition information. A couple grams of fat. A god-awful amount of sodium. Some carbs from the noodles. Added vitamins. Just enough of everything to keep a body going for a while, barely.

Instructions on how much water to add in the preparation directions. Fourteen cans? Usually they only needed one.

Was I supposed to put the water straight into the can? No. It directed me to pour the contents into the saucepan, just like with normal soup.

Except this wasn't normal soup. So what the hell was it?

Under the normal label stuff—nutrition, preparation, ingredients—in print almost too small to read along the bottom of the label, was a tiny legend.

"Warning: *Singularity Ultra-Condensed* uses an experimental packaging method, and is intended only for distribution to qualified high-energy physics facilities. Occasional issues have been reported at the point of delivery that can effect the enjoyability of your meal. If this has happened to you, see reverse."

Okay...

I turned the label over.

In the same small type, in a narrow column, I found a veritable novel.

> *Due to the ultra-condensed nature of this innovative packaging, the product carries with it a slight danger of gravitational collapse. The packaging has been specially shielded and reinforced for your protection against this eventuality. Should your product undergo gravitational collapse, you will recognize the following symptoms upon opening: extreme suction, possible displays of light, ambient wind, possible radiation leakage.*
>
> *Should you encounter any of these problems, close the container immediately.*

Should any household pets get sucked in, do not panic. Simply point the unopened end of the can at a soft surface and open it. Loss of containment will cause objects orbiting the singularity to be ejected out the far end, none the worse for wear.

Upon reclamation of any undamaged objects or animals, simply re-seal the can with available household plastic lids to restore structural integrity of the containment vessel.

Do not attempt to use a compromised product for food, garbage disposal, or time travel. Singularity Soups *can not be held responsible for any attempts to use a compromised product for research or to power any experimental equipment.*

Failure to re-seal this product and return it to the factory indemnifies Singularity Soups, *its subsidiaries, associates, and parent companies, from all liability, express or implied, for any damage to property, persons, animals, the environment, or the solar system.*

This had to be a joke, right?

But when I cracked the lid again, there was light. And wind. And I was starting to get little burns on my fingers.

Well, now, I ask you, what would you do? You're down to your last few meals. You don't have any hope of getting more. You've got your own private black hole, which won't actually eat the things you put in it, it'll just spin them into orbit—I didn't know how that part worked, didn't quite believe it—and which you can get stuff back out of. Hell, all this time I just thought black holes ate galaxies. What would you do with it? What would you think?

Well, I had all those thoughts too. I could take this thing into work, and sneak money out of the till on the sly, and no one could prove I'd done it. I could take it back to the pawn shop and sell it—somebody must want something like this. Who wouldn't want a pet black hole, after all?

But at this stage, money wasn't going to do me much good. Stephen couldn't eat anything but the soup, no matter what, and judging by the way he was today, I'd be lucky to hold on to him through the weekend before he asked for the heroin. I'd already resigned myself to a *Doctor Who* marathon tomorrow, so we could part the way we'd met—cuddling at the back of a room, watching the marvelous magic of a man who never had to die, who always had to leave people behind, who saved the universe because he couldn't bear to miss seeing it unfold.

I couldn't go into work in the morning. I couldn't go out anywhere. I couldn't bear the thought of missing Stephen's last moments. I wanted to hold him when he went. You spend twenty years with a man, you don't wuss out at the end.

My own pet black hole. Any other day, I'd have been thrilled down to the ends of my geeky toes. But tonight?

I just needed sleep.

I SNUGGLED UP, CRADLING Stephen's arm and listening to old *Hitchhiker's Guide* episodes playing quietly on our one remaining computer. I couldn't pawn that—we needed it to stay in touch with siblings on the far side of the world.

His breathing was difficult for a while, but once he settled down, I finally managed to fall asleep.

TEN THE NEXT MORNING brought me kisses. He was strong enough to sit up on his own again, and to stroke my body slowly until I woke up. He wanted to see me play with myself—he didn't say "one last time." He didn't need to. We both knew it. He just said he wanted to see that look on my face when I came, and he wished he could get it up to play with me too. I did what I could to oblige him, for auld lang syne.

We shared a toke. We laughed, as much as we were able. We watched the Doctor change into David Tennant. Only a few seasons left to go till I could let him go—I could only pray he lasted that long.

Still, in the kitchen, there was that little black hole in a soup can. *Singularity Soup* indeed!

During spells where he drifted off, I used the computer to read up on black holes. Hawking radiation. Event horizons. Turns out nothing ever falls straight into a black hole—everything gets swirled around and around forever, getting slowly hotter and hotter, and stretching longer and longer, until it eventually evaporates off. Little black holes are supposed to evaporate fast.

Some people think that black holes are baby universes, and anything that goes in comes out the as stellar dust in another dimension.

But some people—actually, a lot of them—thought a black hole, properly harnessed and shielded, could be used to time travel into the future. Just like the Doctor.

The nucleus of an idea appeared in my head, and it started accreting plans.

That night, after the end of the next season, I made more soup and put in a last pan of brownies. In the kitchen, I kept looking at the label on the counter.

"Hungry tonight?"

"Yeah," he groaned, "Maybe a little."

"Dinner in five." I broke out some clean bowls. "What would you say if I told you I found a black hole?"

"I'd say you've been smoking too much."

"Ha! You would, too." I took the can over to him, and the label. "Check this out."

He pored over the fine print. "Black hole? Asshole, more like. Whoever wrote this is pulling your leg."

"Open it. But be careful."

He raised a hairless eyebrow at me, shrugged, and peeled the lid back. He didn't have much strength in his grip, so as soon as he broke the seal the plastic thing got sucked down into the singularity.

"Holy shit."

"Yeah. Hold on tight."

I ran back to the kitchen and found another lid, then hurried to the bed and slapped it on before anything important got sucked in.

"So what do you do with a black hole?" I asked him.

"Clean the house. Send me off to hell with a clean bathroom."

"Very funny."

Stephen took a hit off hit joint and passed it to me. "Tell you what—throw on another episode. Black hole in the house, we'll pretend it's a TARDIS." He smiled the kind of smile you only see on people who are so tired that they can't summon the energy to laugh.

More soup. More snuggles. More TV.

I thought, and planned.

He drifted off, then back in, had some more to smoke.

Which brings us back to where I started:

Stephen was stoned. More stoned than he'd ever been. Stoned like fucking Pompeii. Like Yosemite National Park. I'd kept him very well supplied with the last of the good bud and the hash oil, because there wouldn't be a tomorrow.

By the time the Daleks took Manhattan, he was so ripped I could have switched places with a woman and he wouldn't have known.

In the closet, I had a stack of space blankets—cheaper than turning on the heating when it was cold—the things they use on space probes for protection against sunburn and superheating. Couldn't hurt, right?

And then some brownies, just in case. I mean, I didn't even know this was going to work, and if it did work I didn't know what it would be like. Best to prepare like a good Boy Scout.

Scissors and duct tape let me make pockets in the space blankets. More duct tape let me secure it.

Once it was done, and he was grinning like he had the energy to play bondage games, I stuffed the pockets with the brownies from the pan. And I got the can of ultra-condensed soup.

"Whatcha doin', man?" He asked me.

"Seeing that you go out in style."

"Cool." He grinned.

Oh yeah, he was stoned. It was only way I could get him in there.

I opened the family-sized can and set it at his feet, and right in front of my eyes Stephen stretched into a ribbon and zipped all the way in. Should be okay, right? I mean, the label had instructions on retrieving household pets unharmed, and Stephen was about the size of a Great Dane. Maybe smaller, with all the weight loss. Only about ninety pounds.

And he had supplies in case his subjective time passed enough that he got hungry.

Well, that was five years ago.

Six months after, they found a new treatment. They could replace the pancreas with a dish-grown one of his own. Without the primary tumor, they could clean up more of the child tumors.

A year after that, they figured out how to locate those teeny little child tumors, so they could actually target them with the radiation—or replace the organs. After the pancreas, all the other organs are easy.

So, it's been four years of saving and eating mostly ramen and peanut butter so that I could afford the treatment for him, and tonight, I bring him back.

Really, Officer. I swear.

I figure he went into orbit around that black hole—he's been gone for a few days, worst case, from his point of view. All I have to do is open the other end and he'll fly out—that's why I need this bed. To catch him, you see? I could never afford anything like this at home, and can you imagine what they'd do to me if I tried this during business hours?

Look, I've got a can opener right here. All I have to do is hook it in like this. Then point the can at the bed, like this, then turn the crank, and Stephen'll come shooting out the other side, good as the day I sucked him in there.

You think I'm full of shit. You don't believe me.

Well...
Watch this.

FUNERAL HATS

IT WAS ALISTON HAYES'S considered opinion that there were very few occasions that the right hat could not improve. Hats added a sense of festiveness to any occasion, even if the occasion was solemn. Once in high school someone had explained to her the appeal of cocaine by saying to her: "It intensifies the stuff that's already going on."

Hats were like that.

For birthday parties, hats made people silly. At weddings, they made people serious. In action movies, they made people dashing.

If you had asked Ms. Hayes to try her best to imagine an occasion or activity that might not be improved by the judicious application of well-chosen head wear, she would not have been able to name one.

This was unfortunate for her, as she did not anticipate that Jac Jarger's funeral would be one such occasion—an error in judgment that led, in later years, to her friends and family referring to the funeral as "The Incident."

THE INCIDENT, OR AT least the lead-up to it, began innocently enough, with the inadvertent murder of Jac Jarger. It's difficult to have a funeral without a murder—or at least a death—and, much as she would have preferred it, it wouldn't have been fair to call Jac's death an "accident," even though he wasn't the intended victim.

Aliston had a friend named Buddy Rich, who she'd gone so far as to marry on at least two occasions, so far as anyone else knew—she decided nobody needed to learn about the most recent time when they'd had a hand-fasting on a camping trip somewhere in the middle of a large bottle of cognac, since it wasn't legally binding—but with whom her relationship had always been...complicated.

She didn't particularly like Buddy, and certainly couldn't stand close contact with him for extended periods, but she did think he was too cute for words, and whenever he wasn't around she missed him in the same way one might miss a mangy neighborhood alley cat who was always having kittens. She felt flattered at having a pet stalker, and didn't mind being caught occasionally, so long as she could wriggle away when she got bored.

It was a game, and Buddy understood the rules as well as she did. She'd had no reason to believe differently, not when they'd played it for so long.

That was before Jac's heart met the pointy end of an icepick which had found its way up through

Aliston's mattress during one of Buddy's hapless burglaries (the kind where he stole copies of her photos, pilfered a handful of her lingerie, and ransacked the whole house just to make the point that he could). If she'd been on bottom, or if she'd been alone, she'd have been the one taking an icepick between the ribs—it was only sheer luck that, on that day, she had picked that particular moment to roll Jac over and do a little dance on his hips while they played.

She'd been called a heartbreaker before, but she'd never thought that the phrase could be so accidentally grisly. Nonetheless, she found herself in the midst of a slew of interviews, flashing lights, and laundry bills that she hadn't budgeted for, all while being down one lover who wasn't a half-bad dancer and was one of the better professors she'd had since she decided to get back into college.

"Accidental death," the coroner said. She hadn't told them about Buddy, having no desire to lose two playmates in one day. Unfortunately, Buddy robbed a liquor store later that same night and wound up on the pointy end of a half-dozen bullets. Karma, she realized, works in mysterious ways.

After that kind of week, Aliston figured that people would forgive her desire for a somewhat festive funeral—if she was stuck helping to plan the thing, which she was, since Jac's children all considered her part of the family, then she *would* find a way to make the day end on something of a happy note. Jac had been a happy guy. He'd have wanted people to leave his funeral smiling.

The trouble with Jac Jarger's funeral started when Jac's sister Trina tried to dis-invite Aliston to the ceremony on the grounds that she was a perfidious bitch who went around banging other people's brothers into icepicks—which seemed a bit harsh, particularly considering that Aliston knew for a fact that, not five years ago when she was seventeen, Trina had drugged Jac and banged him senseless in the back of a car. At least, that was the way Jac told it, and Aliston had no reason to disbelieve him. Trina *was* into that kind of thing, and her friends were all into casting spells and controlling people and stuff, and apparently you upped your sorcery capacity by breaking taboos like they were speed limits. Or something.

Black magic had never really been Aliston's thing, so she'd never really paid attention.

Nevertheless, she *was* Jac's fiancée, and as such it was in her remit to schedule the funeral festivities. It was just a shame the death came so close to when they were to have been married already—so close, in fact, that Aliston had just sent out an amended invitation indicating that the groom would be taking his vows from beyond the grave, and for everyone to dress accordingly. Before then, she still had that pesky hand-fasting to deal with; even though it wasn't legally binding and didn't exactly count, she didn't want to discover that she'd somehow gotten herself damned to hell for being a spiritual bigamist in the eyes of God or something.

That was the first thing that got her down to the pawnshop a couple weeks ago, which had to be the fifth-creepiest thing she'd ever seen, but it was the only place in town she could be sure was going to have the right kind of occult books to do the trick. Trina's friends talked about it all the time, and they would know if anyone did. If you needed a spiritual knot untangled, and couldn't find any good religions, check the pawnshop. What was it Trina said once?

They've got religions down there nobody's even heard of yet.

Or something like that.

Well, they had the books all right. And they didn't want all that much for them. Well..."they" was a run-down looking scrawny guy who had a cat out of a horror movie sitting on his shoulders, but there was a definite "they"-ness about them, like they'd crawled out of someone's conspiracy theory and set up a little pawn shop, like you do when you're fresh out of fiction-land and trying to get a job in the real world with no social security card or anything.

They'd sold her this old-dusty canvas-bound thing with oil and coffee stains all over it, and a little bit of wax and some brown stuff—she didn't know what it was—smeared around the corners of the pages for good measure.

The trouble with breaking the hand-fasting is

she needed the blood of her soon-to-be-ex. That was the key. She needed a thimbleful of it, and then she needed the cord they were bound with—which was easy, since she'd used a bit of rope that usually decorated her summer-weight flower dress—and then she needed to take the blood and mix it with alcohol, soak it into the cord, and then burn it up beneath the full moon.

That took care of half the problem. The other part that vexed her, well, that was trickier. How could you be sure that the man you're marrying is actually marrying you when he's three days dead? He had to actually say the words, right? That was a taller order, and she wasn't sure if using the zombie spell she found in the book would actually count.

But she had to find a way, because, really, if she *was* going to be stuck with someone in the afterlife, she wanted it to be Jac. He was a good man, the kind of man who always wanted to leave a girl smiling. The kind of man a woman might want to walk down the streets of heaven with. The kind that people respected—at least, in public. And then, when no one was looking, he was like the beast crawled out from the pit of hell. It was like having her own personal pet demon. A secret she could always depend on.

First things first, though: She had to be sure that she wouldn't have to be tied to boring-old Buddy in the sweet, sweet hereafter.

So, yeah, it was a bit of a rush job. She had to use a translation site to help her understand the directions she found in the book, but once she got a pretty good idea about what she needed to do she got herself a pocket knife and a sports bottle and headed out to the funeral home where they were keeping Buddy.

While it was true that she'd kept interesting company during high school and the eight years since she graduated, it wasn't the kind of interesting that could have been useful in the current circumstances. Sure, some of their hobbies would even strike cops as interesting, if the cops were well-funded enough to be interested in anything, which they weren't on account of the recession. But none of them were into burglary, or even urban spelunking, which she always thought was kind of a weird oversight, what with all the broken-down casinos to explore.

But, one way or another, Aliston didn't know a thing about how to break into anything, except what she'd learned from the movies, and even with all the movies, she couldn't so much as pick a padlock. So, she figured she had to go in during business hours.

So, the day before The Incident, that's just what she did.

There was a kindly-looking man at the front desk of the funeral home where Buddy was kept. An old man, maybe as old as Jac was, except that Jac was the kind of forty that looked twenty and this man was the kind of forty that looked eighty. She figured he'd caught a bad case of the wrinkles from all the corpses he hung around. Kind of like how people got warts from kissing toads.

She didn't even have to lie to get in—well, not much, anyway. The man was, for example, quite surprised to learn that Buddy had a wife, and wondered why the police hadn't told him. As it was, the dead man's sister and mother had been in already to identify him, and they'd signed for the bill and made arrangements for the funeral, and neither of them had mentioned anything about a wife. Nor had the brother and his wife and their young son mentioned anything about a wife—though he seemed to recall the little boy saying something about "that goddamn bitch" before getting his mouth thumped.

Aliston wasn't phased by any of this. She had as much right to be here as anyone—all those years with Buddy, and the history they had together, and the fact that he'd shoved a big icepick through Jac's heart when he meant to get her, all of it meant two things: First, if she was really honest with herself, he was kind of dim and that was part of his appeal, right up until he demonstrated that he couldn't aim, either. And second, it meant that if *anyone* had a right to see his dead body, it was her. Really, she'd already seen a dead body he *made*, so she should be allowed to see a dead body that he *owned*. It was only fair.

Not that she could say that to the guy at the desk. People in suits were not known for their senses of humor. But they *were* suckers for bereavement, and Aliston knew how to bereave. So, being as subtle as she could, she bereaved at him.

She told him how they'd been estranged, and she'd been in Europe looking for her bliss when she heard about his death. How, upon hearing that he'd met a demise more unfortunate than anything she'd ever seen on those reality TV shows, she abandoned her quest for spiritual enlightenment, left the Dominican convent where she'd been communing with the Dali Lama and his group of Krishna acolytes, and caught the next available train from Marrakesh to this old broken-down town in the Nevada desert.

The funeral director seemed skeptical, but she would not be dissuaded.

No, she wasn't some kind of loony that escaped from the mental bin up the road. In fact, she could prove she was his wife, because she knew for a fact that he had her middle name tattooed across the bottom of his scrotum in a special font that made it look like a black widow spider when the weather was really cold.

The funeral director swayed a little at this, though he seemed amazed at the notion that any of the tattoo artists in this town were anywhere near that good. When she assured him that there was one over by Pete's Meats, and he would totally give a discount if the director dropped her name, he seemed to soften. He even looked like he might say yes, if it wasn't for the police inquiry and the integrity of the body as a crime scene and everything. Did she know about the kinds of things the police said would happen if he let the body out of his control?

Yes, she said, she knew that he was the subject of a police inquiry and she didn't actually want to take the body anywhere, she just wanted to look on his sweet, troll-like face one last time and remember all the reasons they'd been together and all the reasons they parted. Was there any way he could see his way to being kind enough to help her out?

She batted her eyelashes at him, again, as subtly as she could. She thought about all the times she'd lain in bed hoping Buddy would break in and visit her, and how disappointed she got when he didn't show up and she had to spend the whole night alone when she'd been ready to spend her time running around and throwing shoes at him. She managed to coax up a few tears.

Three minutes later she was looking at his cold, dead, slate-gray naked body laying on a freezer tray with a bunch of little shaggy brown-red welts decorating the chest like extra nipples. Some people, she reflected, wore death well, at least judging by the better funerals she'd been to. Buddy...didn't. He looked like a dog that someone shaved bald and left out in the snow. A dog-cicle.

Now she just needed a way to get Mr. Nosy Funeral Director to turn his back for maybe a minute. But she was standing in a big tiled kitchen with one wall full of lockers that looked kind-of like ovens. There wasn't any way he'd believe the "oh, look at the birdie" gag, and when she tried pointing at things and asking what they were he just told her without even looking. She figured he must spend a LOT of time in here with the dead people to catch all those wrinkles.

Given that he was wearing a suit, there was something she could do. It always worked on people who wore suits, because people who wore suits had manners and social skills. So, she thought of the saddest thing she had ever heard of, then doubled it. How would she react if *two* of her favorite TV shows were canceled in the same week just before they answered the will-they-or-won't-they question? That thought was enough to get her sobbing so hard she had trouble remembering why she was doing it in the first place.

But Mr. Suit lowered his head and looked at the floor as if he were praying. Without missing a sniffle, she pulled her exact-o knife and a prescription bottle out of her hand-warmer and sliced a neat little slice into the gray-blue skin over Buddy's ribs...

...but nothing came out. She eeped, and the eep brought the funeral director's eyes up, and she had to drop her hands down near the purple band on Buddy's butt so the director couldn't see them, then she had to explain what had freaked her out. She couldn't exactly say "It's all white in there and there's no blood! He's some kind of zombie!" so she looked around for something to be disturbed about.

Out of habit, more than anything, she noticed how upsettingly like a little cocktail sausage his...cocktail sausage looked, and that proved to be convincing enough. It got the director talking about what death did to the body, about how the genitals got to shriveling up like that because, without the heart to pump it, the blood pooled in the way that gravity dictated it should. Then he pointed at the purple band around Buddy's butt. It looked like he'd been dipped into grape juice.

Three big sobs later, she left the funeral home with a bottle of gloppy blood in her pocket and a great big smile on her face.

An hour after that, she stood in the back yard next to a fast-flaming barbecue chanting words in a language she didn't know at all (and hoping she pronounced them right). The blood-and-alcohol-soaked cord caught the fire nice and easy, and the pesky marriage went up in smoke, so she could concentrate on more important things.

Like hats.

The funeral was tomorrow, and she had to prepare the hats.

There were eight hats to get right. She needed her bridal-widow hat, Jac's top-hat—and a pillow to prop him up in his coffin so the hat wouldn't cover his face because his casket was too short—and the hats for each of the three widowsmaids and widowersmen.

They all needed bows—a good hat needed a

proper ribbon, and for a funeral or a wedding that ribbon needed a bow on it. The wedding colors had been white, navy blue, and slate-gray, and, considering the current state of the groom, Aliston was very relieved she hadn't listened to her mother's advice and picked traffic-cone orange and purple (even though the dresses *had* been too cute for words). Those colors would have been entirely too festive for the somber occasion that the wedding now was, and there just wasn't enough time or money to get new outfits for one corpse, one bride, six attendants, and one venue.

But it was a nice summer afternoon, perfect for a post-witchcrafting crafting session and barbecue dinner, and in short order she had everything put together and ready for work—just in time to be able to savor the sausages. She *did*, at least, remember to wash her hands after she was done with all her work. As much as she loved both Buddy and hat glue, she had no wish to actually add either of them to her evening meal.

Then, with all her pre-wedding responsibilities finished, she decided to do some reading. After casting about for a good book and realizing she didn't have one, she opted for an evil book instead, and settled in on the couch with some Kahlua and cocoa and the fascinating volume she'd bought from the pawnshop.

THE FOLLOWING MORNING began earlier than she normally liked. She had to be up early to get properly coiffed, to pose for photos with the casket and the bridal party, and to see that the final details were attended to. The dawn broke on a glorious and not-too-sweltering day, which meant that she was able to exercise her option—with the funeral coordinator's assistance—to move the festivities out into the abbey's courtyard.

By two o'clock, people had filed in, and filled their seats, and waited dutifully for the festivities to begin. They also grumbled a lot. Her in-laws-to-be were very unhappy with the frivolous presentation, but they showed up anyway on the grounds that they had helped pay for the food, so they were damn well going to eat some of it, considering what it cost, and how Jac's spirit would be disquieted by them making too much of a fuss—but they were decidedly and pointedly not happy about anything there, and nothing that Aliston could say ameliorated their irritation by one iota.

It was only when Trina pointed out that they could all have a family wake—to which they could loudly disinvite Aliston—that they settled down and sat on the widower's side with their arms crossed and their eyes slitted and beady like a row of stoned crocodiles.

Aliston wasn't happy about this, but after some comforting from her maid of honor she resolved firmly not to let their sourpusses darken the bright and happy occasion of her wedding.

She had allowed a few changes to the program. For example, as with a traditional ceremony, the groom began the ceremony waiting expectantly in front of the audience. However, unlike a traditional ceremony, he did not stand expectantly, nor was he expecting to dance with the bride or have a glass of champagne. And he wasn't really expecting anything except to be shoved into an oven after people got done looking at the great makeup job the undertaker's cosmetician had done.

But then, he hadn't been expecting to be killed in the first place, so Aliston figured that just about anything was fair at this stage. He always used to like surprises, at least before the whole death thing came into play. She hoped he still did.

THE WEDDING PARTY came in first. The widows-maids and the widowersmen, arm in arm, step by step, moving forward to the music. The processional was their song, played on the piano (in a minor instead of a major key, in deference to the complicated nature of the occasion) by her third cousin Geoff. He hadn't wanted to play, as he had wanted to marry her a few years ago. She had refused, giving him the polite excuse that he bored her silly and she couldn't imagine an entire lifetime spent under his dour gaze. In truth, the fact that he had red hair just turned her off, and the only time she'd thought he looked remotely attractive was that once when he'd dyed his hair black and dressed up as Dracula for Halloween. Once Jac had died, Geoff had come through at the last minute and agreed to play—a good thing, as their other musician refused to show up on the grounds that he did not play funerals.

After the wedding party came the father and mother of the corpse. They were willing, too. Especially after Aliston had pointed out how she was already on Jac's life insurance policy and that if they wanted any of it they were going to have to behave themselves.

Then, to the great strains of a cheerfully doomy Chopin dirge, the bride made her way to the front. Every step brought her closer to that podium. Every stride, to her beloved. All around her, people dressed in nice clothes, wearing hats to keep off the sun. Some of them even good hats, chosen with taste, whether for a wedding or a funeral, with great bands and beautiful bows and fascinators pinned to trilbys and fedoras and sun hats and spectacular straw sombreros.

And the seats were filled. People really *had* turned out. More than had agreed to come to the wedding. To be fair, yes, the gifts table was looking a little underpopulated, but so many more people had come than expected that Aliston was inclined to forgive small pettinesses like that. They were here, that was the important part. And they would hear what she had to say.

"We have gathered here together to join this woman, and this carcass, in the bonds of holy anthrophagy..." Well, she *had* re-written the ceremony at the last moment, and writing wasn't her strongest suit. She'd had to use a dictionary, and she wasn't sure she'd spelled everything correctly, and now that she was hearing it, she wasn't sure it was right.

But that didn't matter.

What did matter was that, when it was time to exchange the vows and deliver her eulogy, she propped Jac's body up with the pillows she'd hidden behind the coffin stand. Then, unladylike though it was, she sat on the bottom part of the coffin so that she could look her love in the eyes, and she placed the hat on his head.

"Do you Aliston Hayes, take the former Jac Jarger to be your unlawfully deadened husband," et cetera.

Aliston did.

"And do you, the late Jac Jarger, take Aliston Hayes to be your post-mortem wife," et. cetera.

The preacher finished the pretty question, and then screamed. He dropped his ceremony book and dove off the stage backwards, through the flower displays.

The motion distracted Aliston, and pissed her off, too.

Then someone in the audience screamed, which made her look away from the paranoid parson. The distress was moving through the audience, and they were all looking at Jac.

So, she looked at Jac. She met his eyes.

His open eyes.

He said "I do."

Aliston was so excited to see him that, for a moment, she forgot to be frightened. She leapt from her perch and smothered his floppy body and kissed him all over his makeup-caked face. Jac was alive!

So why were people screaming?

Well, when she looked, she saw why they were screaming.

All of the groomsmen (because there *was* a real groom now) and the bridesmaids (because, with Jac alive, she wasn't a widow anymore, even a prospective one), were diving for cover.

Their hats, though, were not. Nor, come to think of it, was her hat. Or Jac's.

All eight bridal party hats flew about in formation like a bunch of sea gulls. Diving, swooping, chasing people over the folding chairs, making people fall over the folding chairs, and generally getting people caught in the folding chairs, sometimes losing their fingers.

Every eye was on the hats. Aliston's eyes were on the hats too, and she forgot to hold on to her husband. She jumped off him and stood aghast as the hats formed up into a face. Six of them forming up the mouth, and two of them forming the eyes.

The eyes looked at Aliston.

The mouth opened. The wind blew through it.

And it spoke.

"Oh sweetie, you brought me back!"

It sounded airy and laryngitic, but it was a voice. A human voice, like whispered through a staticky loudspeaker. A real voice. The kind of voice you could recognize, if you concentrated.

But it wasn't Jac's voice.

"Buddy?"

"I see you! I knew you wanted me, all that time."

Aliston smiled, in spite of herself. How could she begrudge that kind of devotion?

Still, he *was* ruining everything, and hijacking all the best hats besides, and she couldn't put up with that.

"Buddy, this is my wedding..."

"You sent me an invitation."

"I did not!"

"You diiiiid. The blood. The blooood."

He laughed. It wasn't the fun laugh, or the happy laugh. It was the kind of laugh you laugh when you've won a long game because your opponent got stupid. The kind of laugh she laughed at him every time she gave him the slip.

He was *not* allowed to laugh that laugh. Not at her.

"What blood?"

"Theeee. Blooood."

He tossed one of his eyes at her. It landed gently in her hands.

Around the band, the band she'd tied so carefully, if she squinted, she could see the tiniest flecks of dried blood.

"You brought me back," the hat rustled. "Now, you're mine forever."

Oh, no. The game did *not* work that way. She had broken the hand-fasting. She was not going to spend her life shackled to this loser. What would Jac think, having this ghost following her around?

"Jac!" She called. Jac was still at the alter.

So was she, for that matter.

But Jac wasn't moving. He wasn't even breathing. He was about as dead as dead could get, except now his makeup was all smeared and he looked like hell warmed over.

That right there was almost enough to break *her* heart.

But how was she going to get a ghost to obey? If she had the book from that little occult pawnshop...

But she *had* read it. Not cover to cover, but she *had* read it. She just hadn't understood it. Everything was about blood this and saliva that and *herbs de Provence* the other—sort of like someone had stolen Satan's cookbook. She needed someone who knew something about all this occult crap.

And there *was* one person at the funer-wed—or, "haunted church yard," as she had to admit to herself that it had become—that did.

She found Trina cowering in a corner of the garden, a long way away from an exit, with her parents who were too scared to go past the ghost again. Aliston ran towards her, but the hats arranged themselves behind her like a demented hatter's halo, which made her relatives scatter in front of her like pigeons.

Shouting for Trina didn't do her any good. Shouting about money and life insurance didn't do any good. Promising her first-born children if

Trina would just *do* something got a little bit of interest, but not enough to keep her not-quite-sister-in-law from getting dragged, finally, to an exit by two terrified parents who could not understand why demonic hats were suddenly attacking everyone at their son's funeral farce, and why their obviously demented daughter-ish-in-law was running around screaming and leading those hats straight to them.

Aliston needed something that would work. Something that would get Trina's attention. Something Trina wanted enough to brave the Buddy-geist and un-ruin the whole day, even though she hated Aliston's guts and was probably cheering on the inside.

"I'll let you have the book I learned this from!"

That didn't work either.

Trina, along with her parents, found the door and ran from the courtyard. Aliston was now alone with the Buddy-geist, who was all kinds of thrilled that she couldn't get rid of him.

What had so recently been a riot was now a lonely woman standing on a busted-up folding chair looking at a flock of hats in the sky and wondering what she could do about it. All she'd wanted was a good, fun funer-wed. Instead, she had a shambles, and the kind of social embarrassment that was going to make her forever a pariah among anyone who was worth paying attention to.

She collapsed to the foldaway stage, dangling

her feet off the edge. She found herself grumbling about how it wasn't her fault that Buddy got shot, and it wasn't fair that he was going to follow her around forever, and what did he want anyway?

She didn't expect him to answer.

She *really* didn't expect to hear the answer in her own head, like it was his own voice whispering her ear, as soon as her hat dropped back on her head.

"I want to play."

Turning her head, she could see him. She lifted the hat off her head and he disappeared, then she sat it back down again and there he was, sitting next to her, looking very freshly dead and kinda gory everywhere. But still...vital.

Aliston waved her hands around. "What does that even mean?" She had to sniff to keep snot from leaking out her nose, but she figured she was entitled to cry over a disaster like this.

"Like we used to. When we were just kids."

"When you'd spy on me from that tree?"

"Yeah."

"You like to watch."

"It's the best part."

"You can't watch me all the..."

"But I *can*."

That gave her a shiver. A whole colony of them, actually. And not all of them were the good kind.

"Okay, so you can, so what? I still say you can't."

He chuckled.

And Aliston had a serious, serious think.

An hour later, when the preacher poked a nervous head through a well-violated door, she was starting to get an idea. By the time she managed to flee home, she had it fixed firmly in her head. There *was* a way to solve this problem, and give Buddy a good time besides.

As FAR AS ALISTON Hayes was concerned, there were very few occasions that the right hat could not improve. Hats added a sense of occasion to any festival, a solemnity to any party, a memorableness to any social gathering.

Aliston Hayes was known for her hat shop, and the strange charge people got from wearing her hats. A sense of derring-do, a frisson, that lit up every moment with the naughty joy of a four year old wondering if his mother can tell he's been in the cookie jar.

She gave her first, the one Jac had worn at the funer-wed, to the director at the mortuary where Buddy lay in the fridge. Then, because the wrinkled man was so *kind* to her, and allowed her such freedom in the freezer room, she gave one to Trina—herself a perfidious bitch—and a third to Jac's daughter Erin, who had more than a bit of perfidity about her as well.

Word of the hats spread as fast as the hats themselves, and as Aliston's fortunes grew, her fortune grew. Because she always held on to her funeral hat, and she could talk to Buddy when she put it on her head.

Buddy liked to watch people. Aliston liked to

know things.   It was a Jack Sprat arrangement. Together, they made a good team.

A great team.

Or, as Aliston would only ever put it if she ever slipped up at a party because she'd had too much to drink...

A hell of a team.

PICK A CARD

"PICK A CARD. ANY card you like. Don't let anyone else see it." The street performer's carnival-barker-style presentation drew Peter, backpack and all, from the well-worn rut in the concrete that stretched from Rock Island High School to the Hot Zone Convalescent Hospital at the far end of town.

Peters feet had worn that rut all by themselves. Every day, they got a little heavier.

A small colony had gathered around the performer—a magician—on the cold crumbling concrete. The crowd was thick enough that Peter—despite his height—couldn't see well enough to follow the unusual act.

It was a gambler's town. Card games and magicians came with the territory, but normally both things stayed behind the mirrored plate glass of one of the city's aging casinos. The town's pride and sin out here on the sidewalk for everyone else to see? Not normal. Maybe even abnormal. The cops usually busted these scenes up. Peter was never sure if the shows were actually illegal, or if the casino owners—who owned the police department, too—just didn't like the competition.

Kids in school universally held to the latter story.

"That's it, that's it," rang the magician's ragged voice, "now slip the card back into the deck."

Since the magicians all worked in the clubs, and you had to be twenty-one to get in to see a show, this was a chance to get a good look at another magician up close and personal, instead of having to try to catch them on TV specials, where you never could trust that they weren't using editing tricks.

Trying to be as delicate as he could—because the last thing he wanted was to get punched in the face or accused of trying to pick someone's pocket—he found the little empty spaces between the tight-pressed flannel and nylon, and pushed his way in, a bit at a time, till he reached the second row of onlookers.

The magician wasn't one of those crusty gray-haired suit-and-tie white mofos. He had close-shorn woolly hair, the kind of face that looked like he had ancestors from half the countries on earth, and he wore a smart brown leather jacket with orange piping over a slate-blue button-up shirt. Nothing that would claw your eyes out, but the kind of clothes that said *Look here. I know my business, brother, so you'd better take me seriously, or you'll bring the fury.*

The man stood behind a plain table with a

Three-Card Monte setup, two stacks of well-worn antique card decks still in their original packaging, and the kind of confident panache that made him seem to glow, like he was a card-god stepped through from a neighboring universe, and not quite human at all.

But the showman wasn't tossing the Monte cards. He was making a show of shuffling the deck, then stopped and said, "Hold on a minute, how are any of you going to believe this if I'm the one who does it? We need a volunteer...you."

The magician pointed at Peter with the deck.

Peter flushed hot. Suddenly wished he could hide—something his six-foot-three-inch frame never let him do, no matter how much he tried. All those eyes on him, they made him feel as if he wasn't wearing a stitch and looked like a plague victim besides.

Two deep breaths. A couple nervous gulps. Peter stretched out his spindly brown hand and took the deck.

"Fantastic," said the magician.

"So what do I do?'

"Whatever you want."

"Um..that's not very helpful."

"This woman here has chosen a card. Make sure I can't find it."

"But I don't know which card it is and...oh." Peter flushed again, felt like an idiot. But he did know how to shuffle. He'd been into card magic for years. And since last summer he'd been practicing every day. He needed a deft hand at a shuffle for the day when he was old enough to get a job as a dealer at the casinos. Best paying work in town—with all the tips, if he was popular, he could do well enough to pay for a car, and then for college, with just a couple years work. If he was careful and didn't blow it all on the tables himself (an occupational hazard his cousin Wendell had discovered the hard way and never stopped warning him off about).

Peter held the cards in his right, threw little piles of them into his left. Then, with a feel for them, he risked a tent-shuffle, then a one-handed cut, then another tent-shuffle, then another toss-shuffle, then a final tent-shuffle.

"All right, all right," the magician said with a laugh, "enough showing off. Hand them here."

The magician pushed both his sleeves up, showing bare arms below the elbows, then flashed both sides of his splayed hands to the audience, before gingerly accepting the deck from Peter, touching it with his fingertips only.

"Now, ma'am, do you remember what your card was?"

A woman standing in front of Peter, and slightly to his left, whose face he couldn't see, spoke up:

"Yes, I do."

The magician squared the deck off and set it in his open, left palm, all cards face down. He swept his hand under the noses of all those in the front row, so they could get a good look at them. They had taupe backs, weathered-looking, like parchment, with a dove perched on an olive branch.

As he did this, the magician dropped his right arm down to his side.

"Now, loud enough for everyone to hear, can you tell me the name of your card, please?"

"The two of diamonds."

"The two of diamonds you say?"

"Yes."

"Okay, I don't know if this is going to work, but..." The magician's right hand leapt up from his side. Faster than Peter could track, it clapped hard into the left hand, and the two of them pushed forward, as if to scatter confetti into the crowd.

Confetti did, in fact, scatter into the crowd.

Along with a full-sized, properly grown dove, which unfurled its wings and flapped at the crowd, hovering more or less in place, revealing one red diamond on the underside of each wing's pinfeathers.

"Is that your card?"

The woman squealed with delight. The crowd cheered. Peter found himself clapping—he hadn't expected a street performer to be that good, especially this close up.

"Thank you, thank you. And if you liked that, please buy one of these lovely decks of cards. Perfect for all occasions. All vintage. We just got a big load of them and there just isn't any room back in the warehouse..."

Peter looked at his watch. He really did have to get going. He was supposed to hang with Gramp this afternoon, like he did every afternoon.

But every day it was getting harder to make himself go.

And besides, Gramp couldn't tell time anyway. Not with the way his eyes were. He'd have to ask somebody. He wouldn't notice if Peter was five extra minutes late. Or ten.

So he hung around, hoping he'd catch another show.

The crowd filed away. Some buying cards, some not. Before long Peter was alone with the magician-cum-vendor.

"What," Peter asked, incensed on the magician's behalf. "They just gonna all leave you like that?"

"Show's over," he said with a shrug. "Why are you still here?"

"Well I...uh...I guess I just gots to know."

"Know what? Twenty five...good..that's..." He was counting the loot against his inventory.

"How you did that."

"What? Sold twelve packs of cards? With a magic show."

"No, the trick."

"Oh, that. Years and years of practice, kid. Started working on it when I was about...I'd say ten years younger than you."

"Oh yeah," Peter crossed his arms over his chest. "And how old was that? You know, exactly?"

"Seven." The magician didn't even look up.

"How'd you know that?"

"Tricks of the trade kid."

"Come on. I did my first force when I was five. There wasn't any way you coulda done that—she coulda lied and screwed it all up. They do some-times," like those kids at the birthday party Peter had done last summer before he swore off birth-day parties forever. "and there weren't no way it was multiple outs. That ending was too good. So how'd you do it?"

"Squawk all you want, Pete. I'm not telling."

"What? Wait. How'd you know my name?"

The magician didn't even look up. He just kept counting his money. "Same way I know that you're having a hell of a time keeping your grades up while your Grandpa is dying at that sick shack down the road over there," he pointed down past the pawn shop, toward the mountain rising out of the desert five miles distant. Gramp's hospital was dead on that line, another three blocks down. "And your girlfriend is getting sick of you cancel-ing dates on her. She's gonna dump you next week, by the way. Figured it's only fair to warn you."

Peter puffed up his chest. "Hey, man, you been following me?" He wasn't the type to pick fights, but sometimes being tall did most of the work of a fight. Looking badass was almost as good as being a badass in front of someone who didn't know you from anywhere.

The man shook his head.

"So what gives?"

"It's all in the cards." He tossed a deck to Pete while he started packing the contents of the table into a valise living below the fold-em-up rig.

Peter caught the deck, looked at it. For as beat-up as it was—and it was, with white frayed paper spots showing through the threadbare ink anywhere there was so much as the suggestion of a corner in the card-paper box—whoever designed it hadn't exactly skimped on the style. It was all line-art and decco whorls, the kind of over-ornate stuff you'd expect to see in the New Yorker downtown, if they hadn't let the place go to pot with the plaster falling off the fixtures.

"Wow. These must be, like, a hundred years old."

"Yeah, probably."

"Where'd you get 'em all?"

"The boss bought a big load of them off some-one, clearing out an estate. He had a collection. The valuable ones go under glass. The ones that just look cool, he hired me in to move." He started collapsing the table.

"Wait, you haven't sold 'em all yet..."

"Have you *seen* the cops in this town, kid?"

"Stop calling me kid."

"Sorry, *Pete.*" The table broke in half, snapped down on itself, like the magician had released some kind of spring. He set it down on its edge, reached in between two of the folded panels, and pulled out a black plastic handle. "Gotta get going."

One bit of luggage in each hand, he started toward a little parking lot that took up the side yard of the sprawling house the pawn shop used to be.

Peter paced him. "Wait, wait, come on, wait."

The magician didn't wait. Just walked all the way to a broken-down Dodge Dart turned pastered by years of the desert's merciless sun.

Finally the magician said "What? Look, kid, I got places to be. I gotta drop the loot to the boss and get on to this birthday party..."

"Ugh. I've done birthday parties. They suck."

"Yeah, well," the magician heaved the table into his back seat. It barely fit, and took a bit of maneuvering to fit through the door that, to be perfectly fair, was too small for any reasonably-sized human to get into without some serious appendage origami. "When you're doing this for a living, you don't get to turn down a gig just cause it sucks. Look." He slammed the door shut, leaned on the car, looked Pete up and down. "Pete. You seem like a good kid. But I don't got time worth shit even for bad kids. My boss is waiting. Your grandpa's waiting. So bottom line it for me, then you and me can both go get on with our lives and pretend this was just a pleasant little chat."

Peter felt that cold terror grip his heart again, as all the other parts of him flushed hot. Having someone look at him like that, having someone act like something wrong was his fault? That was the kind of look that got followed by fists, and sometimes beer bottles, and long nights hiding up in the tree in the back yard.

And this guy wanted a bottom line? There were about a thousand. Like, how'd he do the trick, and where could Peter learn to do tricks like that? And what about everything he knew about Peter? Stuff he couldn't have gotten from mentalist tricks or cold reads, not in a kazillion years. Peter'd read all the books, practiced it himself. He wasn't very good yet, but that kinda thing took decades and that was okay, but...

"I want to do tricks like that. Like the dove. And that whole cold read thing you did."

"Ah." A mischievous twitch fluttered at the edge of the magician's mouth. He nodded at the deck he'd thrown Peter. "That deck there?"

"Yeah?"

"The trick's in that deck. That very one. Deal yourself a flush, make a wish. It's gotta be a small wish. Big wishes go south fast, don't ask me why. And it's gotta be an honest flush, too. And it only works on red. And it only works once per suit. Two to a customer."

"Oh really. And you wished for master mentalism?"

"Oh hell no." He held up his right hand, showed it empty. Pulled his sleeve up. Pinned his left hand behind his back. Then he snapped his fingers, and fire sprouted from his palm like he'd been holding flash paper—and then the glow cleared, and a rat sat in his just-empty hand. "I asked for real magic. For shows only."

"That was your first wish?"

"No. That was my second."

"What was your first one?"

"Too big." The magician closed his hand. Blood trickled from his fist. Then he opened it again, and his palm was completely clean. "Have fun, kid. And good luck."

If Peter hadn't seen that last demonstration, with his own eyes, and known what to look for, and not been able to see it, he wouldn't have given it a second thought.

But he'd been doing magic—real magic, illusions, not the fairy-tale stuff you read about in story books—since he'd seen his first card trick when he was three. He started out with the rings and matchbox drawers, then moved into cards as soon as his hands were big enough to manipulate them.

And he'd never seen *anything* like that. Never even read about it in a book.

Maybe it was worth a shot.

It had to be a natural deal, the man said, but he could try dealing a stacked deck just to be sure.

It'd give him something to do while he was with Gramp this afternoon.

Good thing too, since Gramp was asleep when he got there and had been since ten this morning.

Boring puke green room up to about three feet, then white up to the ceiling. Cheap linoleum tile on the floor—easy to clean up—two torchiers for mood lighting. An IV tree, an adjustable hospital bed, two folding chairs. The place couldn't have felt more institutional if it had the word Institute in its name.

And Gramp snoring away softly right in the middle of it all.

Peter wasn't sure which was worse—Gramp being asleep, or Gramp being awake. When he was asleep, he looked a lot like he was dead, which he would be soon, no matter what anybody did. But when he was awake, he was pale and weak and always frustrated. He knew how tied down he was, and he tried like hell not to look like it bothered him, but Gramp had been the only man Peter had ever known who had any real sense of dignity. Gramp had taught Peter what the word meant, and that had kept Peter out of a lot of trouble when all his other friends from the neighborhood got all out of hand and into running guns and drugs and trying to make a quick buck.

All the other men Peter had ever known were part of the same world. His Dad, who was dead now. His older brother. His Mom's boyfriends. About the only one who wasn't anymore was his cousin Wendell, and Wendell had gone to work for the casinos because, in his words, he was "too much a chicken shit to strap one on and go fight the man."

And Gramp held onto his dignity even here, even when other people had to wipe for him, and they had him pissing into a bag, and he could barely lift his own arms on bad days. But it cost him, and Peter could see that cost in the red rims around his blind eyes, and the shame they showed anytime he realized that he'd mis-guessed where to look while he was talking to Peter.

It was like watching the Statue of Liberty rusting itself to death. And there wasn't anything anyone could do about it. Just watch it fall down.

But, even if no one else would do it, maybe especially if no one else would do it, he figured he owed it to Gramp to come and hang out with him. Gramp could sleep, and tell stories. Peter could do his homework, as much as he could stand, and avoid whatever loser-of-the-week Mom was following around.

Peter used Gramp's stainless steel tray table, lowered so that it was a comfortable height for the folding chair he sat on, as his desk. But today, instead of homework, he dealt cards.

First he fanned them through, stacked them up, and dealt himself a royal flush of hearts.

Now he had to wish for something. He didn't have any idea what to wish for. But if he actually had two wishes in this pack of cards, he could afford to waste one on a test. Two wishes were like two lottery tickets—twice the chance to lose a buck for no good reason, so why not have fun with it?

Peter held up the pinky finger on his left hand.

"I wish this finger was green."

Nothing happened.

So maybe it did have to be an honest hand.

Or maybe it was just a way for a jerk in a leather jacket to give him the brush-off.

Only one way to find out.

For the next hour, he dealt poker hands. One hand to himself, one into a blind. Then he played both sides of the table, so he made sure he didn't miss out.

He played against himself for points, just so the cards would think there was a real game going.

What the cards *would think? What kind of shit am I thinking?*

Still, better safe than sorry.

When Gramp actually woke up enough to say something, Peter's back was to him. He just about jumped out of his own skin.

"Practicing your cards, Rocky?" Gramp always called Peter "Rocky." Said it was from the Bible, and also a damn good movie. Peter didn't mind—it sounded cooler than his real name, at any rate.

"Yeah." Peter was in the middle of a deal. Moved back to the more sociable side of the table where he could see Gramp.

"Got any new card tricks?" Gramp smiled. It was a warm smile, and a warm voice, but when he thought he was looking at Peter he was actually looking at the wall behind and to Peter's right. Hadn't been so long ago when those eyes had smiled at Peter for real, and actually seen what they were smiling at. Before the strokes, and the heart attacks, and the cancer going everywhere.

"Been working on a new one," he kept dealing. "The multiple outs is getting me, though. I can't remember which ending goes with which twist."

"Show me." Gramp smiled the kind of smile that someone with no poker face smiles when they hope you'll believe them.

"Sure," Pete choked. *God I wish you could really see, Gramp. You'd be impressed.* "Okay...let's see...just give me a sec here..." Pete fumbled with scraping up the unplayed hands. He turned them over to fold them back into the pack and get a proper shuffle going. He had to shuffle upside down for this one to work, at least at this point. He hadn't figured out a better way to keep track of the seven cards he needed to track for this one yet—that came at a later stage. He'd need to learn tactile marking to get the trick down exactly. But for practicing the routine, this was good enough.

"Oh hell." He noticed, after he folded them in, that he'd dealt himself a natural diamond flush. He could've tried his test wish. He'd just have to do it again, at home, sometime. Gramp was awake now, and actually alert, and that didn't happen very often anymore.

"Okay, pick any two cards." Peter fanned them out in front of his grandfather.

Gramps reached for them. Found them first try. Confidently picked one out. Then another.

"I got 'em."

"Okay, memorize them. Do you need me to read them for you?"

"No," he squinted, making a show of it. "No, I got 'em fine, I think."

"Don't tell me what they are. Slip them back into the pile here..." Peter accepted them into the deck, and didn't do any special tactile positioning or marking on them. There were only six cards they could actually be, because of the way he'd handled the shuffle. The technique amounted to a narrow-field force. Really hard to pull off, but really impressive when you did.

He'd been watching as he stacked the deck. He was *pretty* sure that Gramp had the queen of spades and the three of hearts. Now all he had to do was lose all six of the forced cards in a very calculated way, and hide them on himself. That required some sleight of hand that he was still working on.

Good thing Gramp couldn't see. If he dropped a card on the floor he'd be able to sneak down and pick it up.

"Hey, hey what's that move there? You just dropped a card into your lap!"

Peter stopped shuffling. He just about dropped the whole deck.

"Gramp?"

"Yeah?"

"You can see me?" Peter looked into his grandfather's eyes.

His grandfather looked right back. "Well, yeah. It comes and goes."

"But it's been gone for two weeks." Peter's vision was getting blurry. He felt pressure building up behind his sinuses. *Don't lose it, man. Don't start crying like a pussy. Just roll with it. Poker face time. Be cool. It's all part of the show.*

"Has it really? Doesn't seem like that long."

"They've had you asleep for a lot of it."

"Oh. Yeah, I guess they would. God I hate this bed."

"You mean it really worked?"

"What worked?"

"Oh, uh..." Peter flushed hot again. God, he hated having no nerve. Every single stupid time any adrenaline hit his system, he just froze up like that.

But he wasn't going to lie to Gramp, even with a story as stupid as "a strange guy gave me magic cards and I wished your sight back."

Gramp listened the whole time. Really listened. Eye contact, everything. That made it worth the adrenaline. To see Gramp was still *really* there, and that he *really* still cared and...and that he could see again.

Almost like everything was gonna be all right.

When Peter was done, Gramp just said: "Show me another trick."

So he did. He showed Gramp every trick he knew.

And then they played poker. Used to be they'd play for M&Ms, but Gramp wasn't allowed to eat M&Ms, so they played for imaginary M&Ms. Peter kept track of them with a pencil and paper.

Almost until visiting hours ran out. Because God only knew whether Gramp would still be able to see Peter tomorrow afternoon.

"I gots time for one more hand, Gramp, then I gotta go. They're gonna kick me out of here."

"Okay. Deal 'em up, Rocky. Let's see if I can't get your whole pile this time."

Peter dealt. Texas Hold-em. Five up. Two down. No reason to draw things out with card buys when they didn't have anything real to buy with. This kind of game was all about the final showdown anyway.

Pete dealt the table five face up. A ten of hearts, an ace of hearts, a ten of spades, a jack of hearts, and a six of diamonds. One natural pair on the table, a lot of other chances for some mischief, especially playing aces high.

Then he dealt the hole cards, set the deck aside, and picked up his two cards.

And his breath caught.

His hand showed a king and queen.

Of hearts.

Those, plus the hearts on the table, made for his second and final red flush.

He panicked. He couldn't think. He couldn't even remember his name. He didn't want to have to pick a wish, right here in front of Gramp. He didn't even know what he wanted that counted as "small." And there were no takebacks on this. If he wished for something big and it turned nasty, he would never be able to wish it away, or modify it, or anything.

"What's wrong, Rocky? You just turned white."

"I, uh..." Peter put his cards down face up. Looked at Gramp.

"Your other wish?"

"Yeah."

"Well, come on, son, make the wish."

"I don't know what to wish for." He looked at Gramp blankly.

"New car? College tuition? Come on, boy, if this really works, think big!"

"I can't. It has to be small. That's what the guy said..."

"Ah. Small's hard. The small decisions, they're the hardest in life."

"Yeah. Yeah, I'm getting that." Peter thought for a minute. Tried to get his head in order. Everything he wanted was big. The only things he understood were big things. Because all the small things in life sucked, and he just wanted to get away from them, and the only way to do that was to wait another year until he was old enough to move out and work for a living, and then hold on till he was old enough to work in the casinos.

He didn't have anything he wanted that was small...

But maybe Gramp did.

Gramp's world was small now. Maybe a small thing would make a huge difference.

"Gramp? I...um...what would you wish for?"

"That's not the point son, it's not my wish."

"It is. I'm giving it to you."

Gramp looked at Peter for a long time. "You sure?"

"Yeah. I'm sure. Anything you want, as long as it's small. Tell me what it is. I'll wish for it."

"I..." Gramp tried to protest. His eyes were leaking down the sides of his face. Then he breathed deep, and collapsed. "You really will?"

"Yes. Whatever you want."

Gramp nodded. "Okay. I want you to wish that, tonight, Nurse Emerson forgets to turn my monitors on."

"What? But then if you have another heart attack..."

"Then they won't know till it's too late."

Peter couldn't say anything. He just stared at his grandpa.

"I...I'd be killing you."

"Son, Rocky." Gramp grabbed Peter's hand. "It hurts. Everything hurts. And it's never gonna get any better. Please do this for me."

Peter tried to find some way to protest.

But he couldn't.

He'd promised.

So he stood up, wrapped his arms around Gramp, and said, "I love you, Gramp."

"I love you too, Rocky. Go out and kick some ass with your magic."

"I will. I wish Nurse Emerson would forget to turn your monitors on tonight."

"Thanks, son. You'd better go now."

Peter let his grandpa go, gathered up his cards, packed them into the box, slipped the whole pack in his pocket. He gave the old man's delicate, papery hands one last, loving squeeze, then slung his backpack over his shoulder.

He shuffled out of the room, and closed the door behind him.

THE SERPENT AND THE SATCHEL

IN THE BROKEN-DOWN old gambling town border-ing the hot zone at the edge of nowhere, not everyone was suffering gambler's gloom. Some folks–such as the casinos, their employees, and the businesses that served them–hadn't been hurting since the first signs of spring had touched the mountains. The worst was over, it seemed. People wanted to gamble again—at least, people that came in from out of town—and the city's malaise, in certain quarters, had lifted a bit.

Enzo, for example, was doing quite well for himself, at least when accounting by the standards of his modest ambitions. As a displaced Northern Californian of the older sort, he found his greatest satisfaction in being able to make enough money meet his needs while working few enough hours that he could have a life outside of the car dealer-ship at the Palmyra Casino.

This spring brought green back to the high valley that had seemed, for years, to be stuck in perpetual winter. By early May, even the parks set deep in the canyons had given up fighting and started sprouting green. The whole city, and the area around it all the way out to the hot zone, seemed to be calling Enzo to go outside.

He hadn't taken a vacation in over a year, and, looking out the car dealership window on Thursday afternoon, he decided there'd never be a better time.

"Joe!" he shouted as he undid his tie, "I'm taking off the next couple days. Mark it vacation."

Joe tried to keep him around on the grounds that there wasn't anyone else to help him handle the customers, but Enzo left anyway on the grounds that he had the vacation coming and there were four other salesmen around.

On the drive back to his apartment, he rolled down the windows and sang.

Once in his apartment, he stripped out of his work clothes and put on a pair of shorts that were two sizes too long for him, a t-shirt that didn't match the shorts, and a driving cap. He didn't drive anything that really merited a cap, but he didn't have anything resembling hair, either, and he didn't want to get a sunburn on his one and only scalp. He had a fixed notion that people who got brain cancer did so because the cancer snuck inwards from the skin. Protect the scalp and face from skin cancer, he figured, and your brain would keep working as long as you gave it regular oil changes and scheduled maintenance. Or whatever the brain equivalent of those things were. Fresh air, maybe? Hikes? Seemed reasonable—they always cleared his head and made him feel a few thousand percent better.

Enzo strapped on some Birkenstocks and retrieved Monty—his pet ball python—from its terrarium and draped it around his neck. Then, car keys at the ready, he struck out in the general direction of the parking lot, all the while excitedly sharing his afternoon plans with the reptile who, quite honestly, couldn't care less.

FOR ALBERT FREELEY, Thursdays were the worst day of the week. One day away from the ever-retreating weekend, too far from the last one for him to remember what it was like. Boring, too, since nothing interesting ever happened on Thursdays.

Except new deadlines. Thursday was the day that clients decided—at the last minute—that the insurance claims they'd been putting off absolutely had to be dealt with before the weekend. When Albert's co-workers couldn't cope with that kind of pressure—which was every week—Albert was the one who got to clean up the mess. It was in the job description.

Being one of the dullest—or, as he would proudly phrase it, "most dependable"—members of the human race, he'd probably have done that even if it wasn't in his job description. But even so, Albert was convinced that deadlines were called deadlines because they were calculated to give people heart attacks. Similarly, boredom was called boredom because it bored holes in people's souls that other people—usually named "managers"—would later come along and drop dynamite into. Usually in the form of deadlines that threatened to eat the weekend.

It wasn't that he was doing badly, exactly. He had a good job in a down economy, and a family that he liked well enough, at least when he got to see them between work times. If pressed, Albert would even have admitted that, as problems went, boredom and deadlines were the better ones to have. Certainly they was less stressful than divorce and easier to solve than foreclosure.

Normally he dealt with boredom pretty well—boring things were dependable things. "Excitement," on the other hand, was a euphemism for the sort of trouble that usually resulted in deadlines.

Today, though, something was in the air. More last minute projects than usual, more deadlines than he could count on two hands and one foot, all the while the world was turning green and sunny right outside his window. He had the unaccountable urge to throw the entire stack of papers in his boss's face, encourage him to a few obscene and anatomically impossible forms of personal exploration, and storm out of the office never to come back again.

It could work, yes. Delicious, too, to see the look on his boss's face

At least, until Agnes noticed that he was home early and asked him sweetly where next month's rent was coming from. Then he'd have to come back groveling on his knees. At which point his boss would grow horns and a tail and start breathing fire and remind him that his soul was in eternal thrall.

"Albert?" The boss's voice behind him made Albert jump, "Didn't you hear the phone?"

He realized he'd been looking out the window, daydreaming, and immediately started rearranging the papers on his desk. He mumbled "I'm sorry, just trying to get all this stuff put into some kind of order so..."

"Forget it. Forget it. I just wanted to tell you I'm closing the office for the rest of the day."

"But the Constanza report..."

"It's still due Sunday. Just go find a coffee shop to work on it. It's too nice a day to be stuck indoors."

The boss was offering him an afternoon outdoors? Sure. And in the garden of eden, the serpent was just a misunderstood fruit salad aficionado. The jerk was always setting him up to fail, and this time was no different—a suspicion that confirmed itself when, as he was descending the stairs to the parking lot, his brief case handle broke, sending the case and its contents (including his laptop) sprawling down the stairs like so much financial snow.

It took him a good ten minutes to get everything put back together and in the right file folders, then he had to hulk the entire case under his arm like an oversized bundle of schoolbooks. Trying to keep ahold of it while he wrenched open the door of his old SUV was no picnic either.

"Great, now I gotta go buy a new grumble grumble case before I do anything else."

And, his subconscious added, *don't forget, Freddie needs new soccer cleats this weekend.*

No new briefcase then.

But maybe he could pick up a used one?

ENZO DECIDED ON A little park halfway up the canyon. A nice lawn and picnic grounds bordering one side of a deep-forest gorge which housed a modest little creek that, due to the low snowfall this year, wasn't flooding. With Monty around his neck, he tromped for a couple hours up and down the hills, braved the mud flats down in the forest, and eventually found a drinking fountain in a little area with horseshoe courts and volleyball courts and the occasional friendly person walking past.

The whole day felt like something out of community college, one of the days he used to blow off classes and go out to a park for a barbecue and a tennis game and a few beers with friends that were friends specifically because he bought the beers.

Except this time, he had Monty with him, and Monty, being a decent sort of snake, would listen to anything he had to say and never get mad at him for it, so he could just relax and talk about all the cool stuff he'd been seeing lately, like how more people were coming through the dealership, even people who didn't work for the casinos, and how two of them—female ones, even—had asked him out to dinner just this week, and how the weather reminded him that he hadn't called his mother in far too long, and he should probably schedule a time to do that, and how he had enough extra money to get Monty two nice juicy rats this week, and how great the weather was.

Great Thursday afternoons just didn't come around that often, and Enzo was taking all of Friday off as well, so he had to make some plans for what to do with his weekend. Those kinds of plans were better made sitting down where he could do math in the dirt to make sure he wasn't going to spend too much, so he found a comfortable eucalyptus trunk and sat with his back to it, and explained to Monty how road trips worked, and what the ocean looked like, all the while soaking up the gentle late-afternoon warmth filtering down through the forest higher up the mountain.

It took Albert two hours to find a place that carried used briefcases that weren't completely trashed. The sign reading "Lombard Toys and Trinkets," sat unselfconsciously on the roof of an old gray stucco ranch-style home way out on the edge of the hot zone. A second, smaller sign underneath it proclaimed "The finest Pawn Shop in Destelos," which took some stones, since there were dozens of pawnshops in the old gambling town and every single one of them looked less creepy than this repurposed, run-down, haphazardly expanded tract home.

The inside wasn't much to look at either. Stuffed dead animals, intolerably weird art, display cases full of weapons, and a shopkeeper who carried a bald cat on his shoulder and looked like he'd been fired from a funeral home—it was enough to make anyone give up and forget about briefcases.

Except that Albert had deadlines, and if Albert didn't make his deadlines Albert had to file for unemployment benefits.

Besides, driving around on a pretty day had him hoping that, if he made his deadlines and did his work well, the boss might be willing to declare more outdoor work days this summer. Couldn't be a bad thing. Being bored outside was always better than being bored in a cubicle.

Trouble was, the little pawnshop had about a hundred briefcases, and none of them had price tags.

"Tell me what you need it for," the shopkeeper said in a sonorous, velvety voice.

About halfway through Albert's explanation, the creepy young man held up his hand. "Say no more, I know exactly the thing." He walked around the display case and to the briefcase rack, then selected a tan leather satchel with a reinforced cubby in the middle, exactly the right size for Albert's laptop. "Here you are. Something less rigid, something that will remind you to look out the window more. Good solid leather with a thick strap, it won't ever break on you when you need it most. If it does, bring it back and we'll give you a full refund, or a new case."

"A warranty? On a used case?"

"It's all part of the service." The young man smiled in a way that made Albert's skin crawl, but once he was back in his car and on the road to the park, he found he didn't mind so much. When, upon packing his files and computer into the new case, he discovered that everything fit perfectly, he resolved to tell other people about the little store whenever they needed something a little out of the ordinary. A satisfaction guarantee at a pawnshop kinda made the creepy ambiance worth it.

SOMEWHERE BETWEEN balancing his checkbook and explaining to Monty about how gas mileage affected the budget for a road trip, Enzo nodded off to sleep. Not that he noticed—the only difference between his afternoon dreams and his afternoon vacation was that, in his dreams, Monty actually asked the questions that Enzo normally imagined him asking when he was awake. The transition, therefore, wasn't a large one, except that, as the dream went on, the sophistication of Monty's questions grew quite beyond what Enzo expected from the mind of any two-year-old, let alone a two-year-old ball python.

Nonetheless, in the real world outside his dreams, Enzo was the subject of some minor curiosity. A young girl retrieving a ball that bounced away from the volleyball court leaned over him to study his unusual necklace, only to back off slowly and then turn around and break into a run when she realized that it wasn't just thick and pretty, but also moving and flicking its tongue and taking a marked interest in her presence.

After that, the volleyball players pretty much stuck to their patch, and the rest of the park-goers—the picnickers, the families making a beeline for the play equipment, the swimmers intent on finding a hospitable bend in the creek, and the occasional insurance adjuster—walked along the path right past Enzo's sleeping form, completely failing to take any notice of him, or his pet snake.

"YOU KNOW WHAT, Phil," Albert muttered as he looked over two completely irreconcilable repair estimates for one of their biggest clients, "you can just go jump off a cliff, you know? Just go screw yourself, cause, I mean, how the hell you expect me to make sense of this when I don't have the authority to de-authorize an estimate—it's the kind of thing that Kafka used to write about. But I bet you didn't read Kafka, did you? No. Too many adjectives. Too many paragraphs. Not punchy and to-the-point enough for you. Cause let's face it, boss, you get much beyond *Dick and Jane* and you gotta get one of those interns of yours to explain it to you in really small words."

If there were any justice in the universe, Phil

would hear some kind of psychic echo of Albert's words and think it was the voice of God, and then he'd call Albert on the company cell phone and apologize for being an idiot.

There wasn't any justice in the universe, of course, but Albert wasn't disappointed, as he hadn't really expected any in the first place, so he just kept on shuffling the papers on the picnic table, trying to pretend that somehow they could make enough sense that he could email his report in on Sunday.

He'd have to write it at home. The little tumble his laptop took on the stairs at work meant that his only computer was the one he had to share with his kids. But at least he had that—not that it helped him any when he was stuck out here in this stupid park.

Well, stupid but pretty. There'd been a time in his life when he was happy to be in the presence of something stupid-but-pretty, but then he'd married it and found out that it wasn't the picnic he'd been expecting.

Since he'd forgotten to bring any food along, working at a picnic table was no picnic either. The fresh air and sunshine were nice, and when a breeze started up Albert leaned back and smelled the cool, menthol-tainted air spilling down from the eucalyptus higher up the mountain, and the pine and snow higher up than that, and that made things a little better.

It was the kind of day that ought to have a

book. A good pulp adventure novel, like the kind he used to read under the monkey bars in junior high. Danger and derring-do and great beasts and impossible adventures. The kind of story where, if he listened just hard enough, he might be able to hear the growling of some huge, unnameable prehistoric cat-beast off through the thickets.

The rustling noise of the wind in the trees suddenly surged. No longer gentle, a brief tornado-like blast hit Albert in the side of the face. He opened his eyes to see all his glorious organizational work being carried off like so many leaves.

"No no no! Crap! No, stop!" Albert leapt up from his seat and started chasing the loose papers, then thought better of it, skittered to a stop, ran back to the table, scooped all the surviving pieces into a single stack and set the new satchel on top of them, then turned around again and sprinted after the errant pages.

Dashing every-which-way as if he were chasing a barnyard chicken, he snatched one, then another, then another from the air until he had, as far as he could tell, caught them all and stuffed them in a crumpled, rumpled, gangly and unsightly mess under his arms and in his pockets and under his belt.

Park-work should come with hazard pay. There was no way he could include these pages in the report now, not in their sorry state. The xeroxes he could make more of, but the notarized original witness statements...

Well, he'd just have to find some way to make them serviceable again. Iron them, maybe, or have a dry-cleaner put them in a steam press. He'd think of something. He always did. That's why everyone at the office called him "Good Old Albert" and his wife called him "stable" and his kids called him "the best"—when they talked to him at all.

The smell of a barbecue drifted to him. He made sure he had all the papers pinned down this time and checked his watch. Three forty-five, about the time he'd be going for his afternoon coffee break if he were back at the office. He didn't have any coffee here, but he sure-as-taxes needed a break.

"I'd give anything for ten minutes..." Ten minutes of what, he wasn't sure. A good book, maybe. Or the chance to rescue a cat from a tree, or stop a fire—or an alligator—from consuming that group of children over there on the playground equipment. Anything interesting would do, really.

But there wasn't any hope of that. And now that the wind had kicked up, there wasn't any hope of getting his work done either, so he may as well just pick up the satchel and start stuffing...

Albert's hand found a lump in the bag. A lump that hadn't been there before. He felt around—square, hard-sided and leathery, softly serrated riffly sides. A book.

He hadn't brought a book. All he'd brought with him were the now-tragically-dead laptop and the folders full of now-utterly-chaotic paperwork. He didn't remember buying a book at the pawn-shop.

He reached into his pocket and found his wallet, then pulled the receipt from its billfold. It confirmed that he had, in fact, not bought a book there. And he knew it hadn't simply been in the satchel and gone undetected—he'd looked inside it while he packed it in the SUV. How could he help it? The thing was quality workmanship, worth at least twice what he paid for it.

And now there was a book in it?

His thumb and forefinger closed around it gingerly, as if afraid that it would suddenly transmogrify into a dirty diaper, and he pulled it out to discover a handsome, leather-bound edition of *Journey to the Center of the Earth*.

AS THE AFTERNOON ripened, insects came out to feed and frolic and conglomerate in the sunbeams. A particularly gorgeous orange sunbeam filtered through the trees at the top of the ridge and bathed the sleeping Enzo in warm light, even as the canyon around him sank gradually into cooler mid-afternoon shadows. It might have deepened his slumber had not the flying insects harbored an affinity for that particularly brilliant shade of afternoon orange (and, in their attempts to evade the swooping blackbirds that viewed their swarming as a buffet, had not slammed one after another into his face).

Enzo snarfled, then snuffled, then shook and

startled, then swatted sleepily at the air in front of his face until one of the swats landed squarely on his nose. He snapped back, hit his head on the tree, he opened his eyes, and spent a bare moment or two puzzling out why his bedroom looked like a public park.

His memory woke up a few breaths later, and he realized he must have fallen asleep while talking with Monty about the weekend's plans.

Monty. Who'd been happily wrapped around his left arm and draped over his neck. Whose firmly undulating muscles had massaged him to sleep. Whose cool-to-the-touch skin wasn't there anymore.

"Monty?" Enzo reached behind his head—carefully, so as not to startle Monty into a feeding response if he'd slipped back behind to the tree—but found nothing. "Monty, where'd you go?"

Enzo looked at the ground around him to make sure that he wasn't going to step on his friend, then pushed himself to his feet and looked at the sky—the sun wasn't quite all the way past the ridge yet, but it was getting close, which meant that the park would get cold. Monty was a tropical creature—if his body temperature got below seventy degrees, he'd get sick, maybe die. And that's if some parent didn't find him first and kill him with a baseball bat because they mistook him for something venomous.

No Monty at the base of the tree.

No Monty in the piles of fallen eucalyptus bark.

No Monty in the grass, and no distinctive snake-trails either.

No Monty and no snake tracks in the horseshoe pits.

No Monty at the volleyball court.

"Um, mister," a little Mexican girl tugged at his sleeve, "are you okay?"

"Yeah, yeah, I'm fine." Enzo was too intent on the ground to look at her.

"Okay..." She shrugged and turned away.

When Enzo heard her skipping down the paved walk, he stopped, looked back, and his brain caught up with the conversation he'd just had. He'd seen her earlier with a family—at least two siblings around the same age. About six years old, too young to be scared of snakes yet. And kids would look anywhere and get other people on board.

Maybe, just maybe, with her help he could find Monty before the poor guy froze to death.

Enzo scanned the ground for another minute, waiting for her to get to the playground equipment and her pals, then took off after her at a brisk pace, trying his best to seem relaxed and unthreatening.

He got to the edge of the play area and caught the girl's attention when she was at the top of the slide. She zipped down and bounded over to him, but he was careful to step back so that he wouldn't look suspicious to anyone around. He clasped his hands behind his back for the same reason. He'd heard stories about people getting beaten up by enraged soccer moms who mistook bystanders for abductors—and hey, he couldn't say that he blamed them, not in this crazy town.

"I'm sorry about being rude earlier."

The little girl started a bit, obviously un-used to having adults apologize to her. She glowed a little bit.

Enzo continued before the moment passed and she had the chance to find him creepy. "Look, I really do need some help. I'm looking for my pet snake."

"Snake?" Alarm spread across her face, but she said it loud enough to attract the attention of several other children, who abandoned the swings and slides and ran to cluster around her, jabbering excitedly.

Enzo smiled, stepped back, then mimed in the air as he outlined the problem. "He's about this big around, and maybe long enough to stretch from here to here," he used his arm from his fingers up to the back of his neck as a yard stick, "and he's lost somewhere around here. I woke up from my nap, and he was just gone."

"Ooooh," said one little boy, poking the first girl in the back, "He's gonna bite you and eat you all up!"

"No, no, he's perfectly safe."

"But snakes are poisonous!" the little girl objected.

"Not all snakes. Monty's not dangerous at all,

he's not poisonous, he can't hurt you. But if any of you can help me find him and help him, and keep him safe, I'd really appreciate it." Enzo looked over the faces of the children, and saw skepticism. "You don't have to pick him up, just find him and keep track of him and send someone to find me. I'll be looking for him too. But the person that finds him..." he dug into his pocket and pulled out his wallet, retrieved a twenty, "...that person'll get twenty bucks."

The children looked between themselves, voting silently, and then one young boy broke from the pack shouting "I'm gonna smoke all o' y'alls!"

"Nuh uh!" The first little girl bolted after him. "I'm gonna find it. I'm gonna find it!"

That broke the dam. The remaining children scattered every-which-way, scouring the ground for their chance at fame, glory, and enough money to keep them in ice cream for the better part of a week.

With any luck, maybe...

Enzo looked up at the sun, now nearly gone behind the cliff at the top of the canyon. Soon, it would take more than luck to find Monty. He stuffed his hands in his pockets, pointed his eyes at the ground, and kept looking.

JOURNEY TO THE CENTER OF THE EARTH. That was the book Albert read most often in Junior High. He'd read the British translation, and the American translation, and the South African translation, learning all the different ways people tried to deal with the French and German and Icelandic names, trying to figure out which ones were original, then basking in the wonder and the texture of the words.

But the parts that always held him rapt happened in the last half of the book. The adventures with the cavemen, and the dinosaurs, but particularly and most especially the battle of the sea serpents. When Albert was a child, nothing had scared him more than snakes, and all his favorite books centered around giant snakes and lizards and dinosaurs. The alien monsters that really roamed the earth, either now or in the past. The thirty-foot anaconda, the giant cayman, the mere thought of them made his blood swirl in little nauseating eddies. Deep down in his secret heart, he couldn't get enough of them.

Albert looked at the paperwork, now half-stuffed into the new satchel, then at the book in his left hand.

He looked between them again.

To anyone else it would seem silly. But to him, today, in this park, it was a sorer temptation than cold beer on a hot day when he hadn't had a drink.

He couldn't take the time. He had to get home where he could work without the wind screwing him up, so he had some kind of prayer of meeting his deadlines.

Albert set the book down. He stuffed another handful of disheveled file folders into his satchel, reached for the last stack, and his hand brushed the book again. He started. He stared at the cover, with its simple gold leaf design embossed on the leather, and those magic words luring him inside. Somehow, he was having trouble remembering to breathe. His heart stung, just a little. He felt hungry and tired and brand new to life all at once.

Off to his right, nobody was looking.

Off to his left, nobody was looking.

Stealing a glance behind, he couldn't see a soul. Certainly not anyone who'd care.

He couldn't see anyone at the top of the bluff behind him.

Peering forward, stepping up on the picnic bench, he couldn't see anyone in the forest.

Nobody around. Nobody to care.

Albert quickly rehearsed all the reasons why he shouldn't pick up the book.

After running through the whole list, and failing to find a single one that he cared about one whit, he pushed the satchel to one side, dropped the remaining files on the table. He seized the leather volume, parted the cream pages, and searched for the sea monster battle.

The golden sunlight made the pages glow in his hands, and the story pulled him in just like it always did. Before his eyes the giant battling sea serpent sliced the waters like a whip, then twisted back on its ancient enemy like a wriggling worm.

He could taste the salt of the underground sea air.

He could smell the blood and the danger.

He wished he'd brought a harpoon so he could join the battle himself.

Some time later, after the book's hapless heroes had cheated death yet again, Albert was startled from his pages by a flood of children running past him, urgently making toward a family across the lawn to his right.

A little Latina girl reached the family first—a couple with children of their own, attempting to dig into an early dinner—and shouted "There's a big monster snake on the loose and we're trying to find it!"

The little boy with her added "Yeah, a mean one! And there's a reward and we're gonna find it and catch it and..."

"And..." the girl interrupted, "will you...um...will you help us find it?"

A big monster snake? Albert felt the hairs on the back of his head stand straight up.

The couple looked at each other, picked up their children—leaving their food—and hot-footed it off the lawn and down to the bridge across the deep creek bed.

"Great move, dummy," said one of the boys, hitting the girl on the arm, "What are we gonna do now?"

"We'll just keep looking. He's gotta be here somewhere, right?"

Albert looked back at the book. His favorite Earth-center-seeking heroes wouldn't have shrunk from something as trivial as an escaped giant snake. They wouldn't have broken into a sweat at the mere thought. No! They'd have seized the day with a machete and a pith helmet and a bullwhip and a spirit determined to seek and find and conquer any obstacle, no matter how great!

Of course they would. That's what made them heroes.

Albert let his breath go, his shoulders slump. He was no hero. He was just an insurance guy. His whole purpose in life was to make sure that nobody cheated, or got rewarded for unnecessary risks. Dashing adventure wasn't in his character.

But maybe...

Just maybe...

The difference between a hero and an insurance guy was exactly this: which one had the courage to find the giant snake? Maybe anyone could be a hero if they stared the snake in the face and showed it who was boss.

Albert straightened up.

He would find the snake. Yes he would. He would find the snake or die trying.

He reached into his satchel, and his hand found a machete. It rang as he drew it out, its blade glinting gold in the day's amber light. He reached in again, and found an intricately braided coil of leather. He drew it out. A magnificent bullwhip, twenty feet long, handmade, and tapering from a free-spinning mahogany handle.

His hand went in again, and drew out the final

bit of his adventuring kit, the crowning tool of any adventurer going into danger:

A pith helmet.

Albert stood up and placed it on his head. As he did, he could swear he heard swelling music trumpeting the commencement of his quest. He felt taller, broader, like a man of bronze standing guard over an ancient harbor. Today was the kind of day people would make movies about.

The machete went onto his belt. A sheath specially made for it hung there. He seized the whip in his right hand, lifted his left to his helmet-shielded brow, and scanned the horizon.

"If I were a monster snake," he muttered, "where would I go? I'd want enough cover to lie in wait, enough prey to stay fed. I'd want shelter, a place to look out from." Albert scanned right, faced the forest lining the lawn, and the gully it plunged into. "Yes. An ambush. The perfect cover!"

Albert planted his left foot on the bench and leapt over the table. He landed near the edge of the forest with his coiled whip at the ready. The gully wall sloped away at nearly ninety degrees, and it was all crumbly shale. No way to climb down—there was only one solution.

He tossed the coils out to the side, swung the bullwhip in a wide arc to pick up momentum, and then, easy as breathing, flicked it forward to a low-hanging branch about ten feet distant.

The leather thong twirled around the branch.

The end slapped, and bit.   Albert tested his weight—the whip stayed stuck.

He took a deep breath, ran in a wide arc at the edge of the gully, and pushed off into the open air. Trees and branches and vines whizzed by as he swung, heading lower, lower, down toward the deep mud flats overgrown by bay and cypress and grasses of all kinds.

Ahead of him, he spotted a weathered gray stripped-down tree, its old limbs jutting out like a pincushion. And he was flying right at it.

His feet met the dirt at a run a couple yards from the tree. Albert dug the side of his boots in, slid down into the mud as if he were stealing second. He smashed to a halt against the trunk of the tree, his face mere centimeters below a sharpened limb that almost impaled him under the chin. It did, in fact, take his hat—the pith helmet was stuck end on at the end of the limb a few inches away.

His breath slowed. He rolled out from under and found his feet. He brushed the mud off his legs—bare below his safari shorts—and the side of his torso. His khaki shirt would need laundering, for sure, but wasn't that a given when you're going into the jungle to hunt the great beast?

The hat, though.   The stiff brim of his helmet was impaled—properly, well-and-truly skewered—on the end of the low branch.   On close inspection, Albert found that it wasn't just naturally sharp.   No, it had been deliberately sharpened and scorched by human hands. With a pocket knife, maybe, or a flint tool. The cold realization washed through him: There were other hunters on the trail, and they were ahead of him, and they did not want competition.

Well, that might be. But they hadn't reckoned on competing with Sir Albert of Freely, the greatest hunter in the modern world.

Albert plucked his helmet from the branch and settled it back on his head. With an easy flick of his wrist, he released the whip from its anchoring branch and curled it up with practiced expertise. The time for whips was over. He was heading into the undergrowth, into tracking territory. Time for another weapon entirely.

"EXCUSE ME, SIR? You, in the bushes. Sir!"

Enzo stood up out of the thicket and looked around. When he saw the two Park Rangers on the path, alarm set deep in their faces, one of them with his hand on a gun, his heart sank.

"Yes, officer?"

"Are you the man who lost a snake?"

"Yes sir."

"Are you aware that it's illegal to keep endangered species in this state?"

"What? Who, Monty? An endangered species? You're kidding, right?"

"A thirty-foot anaconda..."

Enzo laughed. "No, no, no. He's a ball python. Little guy, about like this," he mimed Monty's dimensions, "completely harmless. I just don't want him to freeze, which he will when the temperature gets down below seventy. Wait...who told you he was an anaconda?"

"We got a distressed call from a mother whose son was..."

And so on.

JUNGLES. THE UNTAMED wilderness. In the days-long quest so far, Sir Albert had survived an encounter with cannibals, a bout of dysentery, and an attack by a hungry tiger. His wounds were deep, but healing under the banana-leaf poultices that he'd gotten from a friendly medicine man.

The medicine man had had his own tale to tell.

Something terrible was going on in this jungle, and Albert knew what it was. The small creatures, all of them, had been devastated by the ravenous appetite of the giant serpent. Children also had gone missing. All of the other predators were growing wilder and more aggressive. The monster had to be caught, or the jungle would plunge into chaos and darkness.

And now, after all his searching, Albert had found its trail. Unmistakable. A deep, strafing, crescent groove in the wet sand on the bank of a brook. The undeniable track of an enormous snake, bigger around than a truck tire, easily forty feet long, maybe longer. A leviathan capable of terrorizing the countryside for decades.

Albert ran his fingers through the track, trying to get a feel for the creature. The track ran forward to the far bank, then off into the underbrush. It was fresh, too. Even under the water, the impression was clear and true. Not more than a day old, and probably much fresher still.

His machete sang as he tore it from its sheath. Albert launched himself across the water and ferociously tore into the vegetation on the far side, hacking a trail through the impenetrable undergrowth. The thorns and tares scratched at his face, sliced at his legs, dug into his boots. But he persisted. He endured. The track continued at his feet, he would follow it wherever it led.

His tired arms found an easy rhythm through the vines. A figure eight, hard down left, up and around, hard down right, sweep the detritus out of the way. He made good time. Nearly twenty yards every hour. The track continued infinitely in front of him.

From time to time he nibbled on fruit he'd picked and stuffed in his pockets, and on pangolin he'd smoked over a fire a few hours back, but he dared not stop. He could feel the jungle closing in behind him. The predators, starved for their normal meals, could smell the blood and sweat, could hear the ching-ching sing of the blade as it carved his path through the wilderness. He could hear them, growling, fighting, just out of sight. Only the thickness of the undergrowth, and his constant motion, protected him now. And, if it came down to it, his machete and whip.

Then, as if the world had thrown a switch, the last of the thicket fell away to reveal a wide flat riverbed with only the barest of dry-season trickles flowing along it. The beast's track continued off to the right, joining the direction of flow and continuing down it.

Albert's fatigue lifted from him. His fear evaporated. The ground was firm, it was open, and he was on the scent! He broke into a run, harder than any Olympic marathoner. Sir Albert, running like the wind, chased the great leviathan through the jungle.

The sounds of predators faded behind him as he ran.

The thick, humid air poured into him like honey as he ran.

His feet crushed the mud beneath him, etching his tracks for all later hunters to see how he ran.

And as he ran, the snake's trail grew fresher, and faster, and bigger, and more detailed.

A monster indeed.   And he was hot on its heels...or, well, tail.

Then, a scream ripped through the jungle about him. The kind of scream that hooks its claws beneath your ribs and rips your guts out.   The kind of scream people only make when they're being eaten alive. The kind of scream that ends in gurgles.

Albert slammed to a stop. The screams weren't coming from farther down the track. They were coming from behind him.

Behind him.

He'd passed a little tributary not a hundred yards back. Was it possible the beast had circled back around?

He didn't have time to think. The screaming was fading—whoever was making it was dying. He had to act decisively, and quickly, as all good heroes did.

Albert abandoned his quest—only for the moment, he promised himself—and set himself to running again, this time in the direction of the screams.

ENZO MANAGED TO convince the Rangers that he hadn't brought a dangerous animal into the park. Once convinced, they even agreed to help. First, he took them in a review of the ground he'd covered, being sure to steer a wide berth around the poor man in the office clothes who was sprawled, sleeping, across the papers on the picnic table over by the edge of the gully.

He started with them where he had started, and quickly ran them over all the ground he'd covered. He filled them in on the habits of ball pythons, and the kinds of things they liked to eat, and how they were really very shy and prone to curling up in a ball to avoid attention, hence the name.

Then, once the Rangers were on the hunt themselves, Enzo jogged back to where he'd personally left off, and resumed calling Monty as if he were a dog.

He knew snakes didn't exactly have ears, and couldn't exactly hear, but Monty was a special snake, and if any snake was nifty enough to be able to hear its own name, it was Monty, so it was best to be on the safe side.

"Monty! Come on, buddy, we gotta go home. I'll get you a nice juicy rat, fresh, too. Promise. Come here, boy. Monty!"

THE TRIBUTARY ENDED at a spring in a head-high rock outcropping.

The stream flowed red with blood.

A little ways up the rock, Albert found a sneaker, tossed aside, without an owner, but not without a foot. A bone stuck up out of it, and blood ran from it. And in the grasses above the little stream, the signature mark of the beast, the strafing swirling tracks of an unspeakably humongous python. Probably a world-record holder, as it had to be big enough to eat a human of not-inconsiderable size, with jaws sharp enough to sever the foot at the ankles. Not normal behavior for a snake, but then, this was no normal snake.

Albert took a moment to weep over the shoe. He had failed to save the life of an innocent. A pedestrian, just a hiker. Someone with no stake at all in the great contest between hunter and beast.

"I will avenge you," Albert vowed through his bitterness. "The jungle will be safe again. I swear it, by almighty God and all his angels, I swear it."

He had to be close now. This blood was fresh. Hadn't even coagulated. The after-echoes of the screams still rang in Albert's ears.

"That *beast*," he said, "That beast is mine! I shall have it mounted on my hearth by the time night falls!"

He sprang up the little rocky outcrop and stood on ground cleared by the recent struggle. Ahead of him, a narrow groove stretched for a dozen yards before disappearing around a tree, so fresh that grasses were still springing back from the compression. He followed it, and when he rounded the tree...

He saw it.

There, laying lazily on a limb in a sunbeam. A giant reticulated python, old as the very rocks and twice as ugly. Thick around the middle with its recent kill. Its tongue flicking out, catching his scent, looking back and forth for threats. All forty-five feet of it, with jaws as wide as a man's shoulders. The most enormous snake Albert had ever seen.

But he did not falter. He did not quail. Albert shifted his machete to his left hand, seized his bullwhip in his right hand and deployed it. He hunkered down into a wrestler's crouch and growled the kind of growl that would frighten tigers away.

From beneath his pith helmet, he glared, and stalked, and approached his prey.

The beast saw him. It turned its face and locked eyes with him. Such a snake could strike more than a third of its body length—every hunter knew that—but in order to pin it with the whip, Albert needed to be closer than that. He needed to be within ten feet.

The snake reared back.

Albert stepped in range.

The snake struck.

Albert was ready. He dodged aside, just barely saving his face from being smothered by the white envelope filled with thousands of teeth. He lurched back toward the snake, trying to grab around its neck to subdue it, so he could chop its head off, but the snake withdrew too fast.

It was on him again. This time it caught his shoulder, but Albert yanked away, losing a chunk of muscle in the process. He howled. Around him, the jungle howled in sympathy.

Back and forth it went—strike, dodge, bite, escape. Albert's only hope was to tire it enough that he could lasso it with his whip.

Then, a stroke of luck! The snake struck at him, he dodged, and its teeth caught on a branch. Albert didn't hesitate. He flicked his whip and snapped it easily around the creature's neck, binding it irrevocably to the tree it had inadvertently bitten.

Victory was his!

But the python had other plans. As Albert laid his hands on the python, its massive body slammed into him from behind and wrapped its cold, dry mass around him. His arms were pinned. His breath squeezed out of him. He had no hope at all, unless...

Yes! He still had his machete. He turned the blade outward, where it touched the reptile's scales, then, using what little mobility and oxygen he had left, he started sawing it against the creature. At the first prick, the snake tightened. Albert felt the warm blood gush out across his legs as the machete bit into the leviathan's flesh.

Tighter. Tighter. Further, further. Albert's lower body was soaking now. His vision was starting to go. With one last herculean effort, he yanked his arm upwards, dragging the steel blade with it.

The machete won through the guts and into the spine. The snake shuddered, and loosened the tiniest amount. Albert sucked in fresh wind and redoubled his push, working his other hand around to the back of the blade and using it to push.

Push.

Push through!

The machete won through the bone.

The steel pushed through the skin on the far side.

Fifteen feet of monster snake fell dead and twitching around his legs.

The upper part of the monster flailed and flapped in fury, its body heavy as an elephant wielding a club. Albert dove for the safety of the earth and wriggled out of range, the dead end of the animal still clinging and quivering around his legs.

He looked back. The beast was flagging, its remaining blood spraying the green forest crimson.

Albert struggled to his feet, hanging half off a tree trunk in his exhaustion. He kicked the beast's tail away in disgust, and then, after taking in a deep breath, bellowed his triumph.

His voice echoed throughout the jungle.

ONLY ONE FINGER OF sunlight still penetrated the canyon. It fell on the shape of a twitching, sleep-talking insurance adjuster with a tan satchel, a sheaf of scattered papers, and a handsome copy of *Journey to the Center to the Earth* on his picnic table. The book, stuck as it was under his face, was taking an unholy soaking in the drool department.

To his right, a curious little animal was investigating the scent of his fingers. It wasn't more than four or five feet long, and no thicker around the middle than a tube of toothpaste, and its little tongue was all it had to smell with. It hadn't eaten all week, and feeding day was tomorrow, but the day so far had been filled with such a powerful variety of new scents and textures that nobody would begrudge it a little nibble. At least, if it could find something to nibble on.

The fingers, though, weren't looking quite so good. Even though they twitched like mice, they seemed to be connected to something altogether bigger and more indigestible. It smelled like laundry soap, too, which wasn't a taste that the little creature was fond of in the least. It gave them up and struck out in the general direction of the big round furry thing about half a body-length away.

When it got to the big furry thing, though, the entire table jumped.

It jumped because, when the snake's little tongue hit Albert's ear, Albert's entire head shot straight up in an attempt to get to the moon as quickly as possible, and Albert's body wasn't far behind. The little snake curled up in a ball, and Albert screamed:

"Bwah! Oh my god! Snake!" He stepped back out of range and darted forward as fast as possible, snatching first the satchel, then some papers, then the book to his chest. Then, on the grounds that the insurance clients could jolly well jump off a cliff, he abandoned the table and ran, hugging his luggage and stray papers to his chest, along the paved trail toward the park entrance.

Enzo was still looking for Monty, this time at the wooden bridge over the gully that led to the parking lot. It was the kind of place that Monty might want to catch some sun. It was mottled and would provide good camouflage, and it soaked up the day's heat as well as any rock. But so far, nothing.

He had to go slow, though. Ball Pythons blend in well, and he couldn't afford to overlook Monty. He couldn't have his little friend dying out here.

"SNAAAAAKE!!!!" A man's voice bounced off the canyon walls.

Enzo snapped to standing in time to see a harried-looking office worker, running at full speed and streaming loose papers behind him, stumble at full sprint onto the bridge. He regained his footing, regained top speed, and barreled straight for Enzo, looking him dead in the eyes and waving his arms behind him like a wild man. "SNAKE SNAKE SNAKE SNAKE SNAAAAAKE! AIEEEEE!!!!!"

The man zipped past. Enzo tried to catch him, but he was too fast, so all Enzo could do was watch the man go. At the far end of the bridge, the last of the man's luggage flew up and over the railing and into the gully, but the man didn't care. He just ran headlong into the front of a parked SUV, felt around to the driver's door and yanked it open, then backed out, turned around, burned out his tires on the way to the exit.

"Snake?" Enzo said. "Snake?! He found Monty!"

Enzo turned around and ran as fast as he could. He was pretty sure that was the man he'd seen sleeping earlier at the picnic table. If Enzo was fast enough he might just...

Yes! Monty was still there on the picnic table, just uncurling from a ball of alarm.

"Monty! There you are!" Enzo swooped his little friend up into his arms and kissed it. "I was so worried about you! Where'd you get off to?" The last of the sun disappeared over the bluff. "Looks like I found you just in time. Come on, let's go home. I'll give you an extra rat this week."

Enzo straightened the serpent out and draped it over his shoulders like a gym towel. The ripply cool muscles pinched and relaxed like a portable neck rub. Monty was happy with the heat, and Enzo was happy with the neck rub, and that was the entire basis of their relationship. A good relationship too. And tomorrow, they'd drive out over the mountains and Enzo would show Monty what an ocean looked look like.

The man and his pet shuffled across the bridge and got into their car, and, together, they drove off into the sunset.

And the satchel from the pawn shop? It stayed in the creek bed for a couple months, until a fifth-grader happened upon it. And trust me, he really needed it.

THE END

Turn the page to read a sneak preview of
A Ghostly Christmas Present
A Madness-filled Holiday Mystery from J. Daniel Sawyer

Sample of

A Ghostly Christmas Present

6:00 PM, Sunday

Clang.

It's a special sound to hear on Christmas Eve morning, more distinctive than any Salvation Army bell. Immediately before you hear it, some gruff guard is liable to bellow out an "all clear"—but I wouldn't count on it. Like cops, prison guards come in two flavors: the compassionate ones that wanted to make the world a better place, and the abused kids that grew up to be bullies. Cops—well, cops in well-run departments—tend to tilt toward the former. Prison guards tend to tilt the other way, so if your hand gets crushed when the gate closes, it's more entertainment for them.

They sure as hell didn't know what to do with me. They kept looking at me and saying "you don't belong here," even during the strip search.

Of course, in this podunk Twin Peaks wannabe town, the sheriff's deputy that threw me in here claimed they didn't have any room left in the holding tank because of too many drunks. Besides, I used to be a cop. I'd be fine in lockup, right?

Yeah, right.

Naturally, they stuck me with the big mean-looking dude who would've been called "Bubba" in any prison movie. That he introduced himself as "Manny," and had about a third grade education, gave the enterprise just enough pathetic to keep me fighting back my menacing laughter.

"You an' me's cellies now, boy." On anyone else, that squeaky voice would be a dead giveaway that his balls were just starting to drop, except this guy was easily twenty five and, judging by the swastika on his shaved head and the Black Power tattoo on his left shoulder, a confused victim of identity politics. Hearing him schlep up behind me like he expected me to beg his favor wasn't one of the more companionable roommate experiences I've ever had, and I went to school at U.C. Santa Cruz. "You's gonna be my good boy and I'll make sure life is real purdy for ya."

I heard fly buttons pop open behind me. In jail for fifteen minutes, and I already got an overgrown third grader trying to play doctor with me. Joy to the world, my cell-mate wants to come.

I stepped back from the bars until I bumped into him and said, in my best quavery scared-as-hell coward voice, "You promise? Thanks, man." I reached back 'til I found his hip, snaked my hand down to his balls, and got a good handful. Then, I gave them a nice squeeze and a slow twist.

"Ooh, that's right boy, jes...ow! What the..." I clamped down so hard he couldn't do anything but grab the bunk and try to stay upright so I didn't take his nuts off if he fell backward.

Another really good twist, and a little more pressure, I turned around to make sure I had his undivided attention. "Oh come on now, Immanuel. I'm not your captive." Yeah, I was in that kind of mood. Endless Christmas music in hotel lobbies does that to me.

He squeezed out a "Huh?" between groans and failed attempts to scream.

"So here's the deal. We're gonna be pals. You and me, all the way. But I ain't your catcher, or I'll take these," I gave his jewels another twist, "and make 'em into a necklace. You got me?"

Staring down a guy four inches taller and a couple hundred pounds heavier than you isn't exactly a trick you learn in kindergarten. Time on the beat has its advantages.

He gritted his teeth. Sweat beads coming up on his head now. Face red as Rudolph's nose. Kept him in too much pain for the adrenaline to help him any. Good thing too—he could've made a smoothie out of me without trying. But after this much pain, I was banking that he'd need to sleep off the testicle torsion before he got his revenge. A bit of a gamble: there weren't any scheduled activities for a couple hours yet, so I was stuck in here with him.

And he wasn't answering my question.

"I said," I scooted close enough that he tried to retreat. Coach, we have a first down. "Do you got me?"

He still didn't say anything.

"Look, if you don't answer me, I might just have to blow you. And I haven't had breakfast yet today." I squeezed a little harder. Much harder and I might actually break something. "So, you got me?"

"Yeah, yeah, goddammit, I got ya," he squeaked.

"Good man." I let go all at once and gave him a gentle push. He collapsed on the bed with his hands cradling his genitals, and curled into a fetal position with his ass hanging out of his drawers.

Well, there was gonna be a full moon tonight. Might as well start early.

I turned my attention back to the view out the bars and ran over my less-than-dignified Christmas Eve.

Count on the idiot named "Clarke Lantham" to provoke a cop just because the cop was a prick. Count on him to do it in a state where his lawyer wasn't a member of the bar, and the only person he could call was the brother whom he'd deliberately avoided telling he was in town. And then, count on that same self-professed idiot to do it all when he was trying to get home by rental car to see to a business emergency.

Yeah, there's some things only the ass-end of a set of prison bars can teach you. Chief among them being: "Don't try to find a way out of Sea-Tac through the suburbs when a snowstorm closes the airport."

Granted, it isn't the kind of fortune-cookie proverb that's likely to come in handy every day, but if the waitress at the Hilton had been kind enough to scribble it on my receipt this morning I'd be at least a whole mile south of the airport by now, without having the extra helping of testicles before lunch.

If I'm gonna be honest, though—and, when you're standing in a prison cell with a four-hundred-pound six-foot-five cellie snoring like a polar bear with flu, there isn't much sense in creative self-deception—my assistant Rachel pegged my first mistake during our phone meeting yesterday. Her typically genteel appraisal of my situation ran something along the lines of "Jesus Christ, Lantham, only you would go to an insurance convention in Seattle in the middle of inheritance season and not check the weather report. How the hell did you stay in business before you hired me?"

She was gonna crap fresh grapefruits when she heard about my current predicament. Top of my agenda was not letting her find out yet—last thing I needed this morning was guff from my twenty-year-old underpaid gothy employee. Particularly when she was right about it.

Now I just had to wait for my brother-who-wishes-he-wasn't to show up, and ponder the meaning of Christmas—which was ostensibly coming tomorrow, though the weather seemed to have different ideas.

I can sum up the meaning of Christmas in one word: Crunch.

Otherwise known as "the sound you don't want to hear when you're in a car."

For me, the holiday season is full of little surprises from Santa like that one. Most years, I'm home in Oakland, and December in Oakland is a miserable thing: In bad years we'll get ten or twelve inches of rain over the month, and the thermometer will drop to forty degrees during the day—sometimes we'll get some frost overnight. It's a horror show for traffic—the interstates can get so bad that it might take more than an hour to make the fifty miles from Oakland to Los Gatos.

If you live in the Bay Area, you learn to hate it. So the thing about winter is really that, when you live around the Bay, you forget what the thing about winter is. You think about the rain and the minor bump in traffic. You think about what a pain in the ass it is to have to remember gloves if you're going out after dark and intend to spend any amount of time outside (and really, who goes outside in winter after sunset for any reason other than to get from the car to a club?). You get to think that these kind of piss-ant conditions actually constitute "bad weather."

With that in mind, you probably think the reason that the side of my car was mushroomed in from a broadside in the Seattle snow was that I blew through a signal at ten miles an hour on slick ice, right?

Yeah, you'd think that. It hurts when reality doesn't cooperate with prejudice, isn't it? I run into that all the time.

Sorry for the surly mood. It's been a hell of a few days. But rest assured, I keep my cold-weather knives sharp with twice-annual refresher courses at Infineon. Have to. My PI license means I can operate anywhere in California, and you never know when someone's going to call you up to Dodge Ridge or Tahoe to find their missing cat.

So yeah, I am spoiled rotten, but I also live in California, and I'd have an excuse if I drove like crap in the snow—even though I don't. The mooks up in Washington, though, who get snow at least once a year, act like they've never seen the stuff. White flakes start falling from the sky and they all rush out to the store at sixty miles-an-hour to buy God a fresh bottle of Head and Shoulders.

Of all the sounds that can tickle your ears when you're in the car, "crunch" is right up there with "boom" for ones you don't want to hear. But it's *really* not a sound you want to hear when you're sitting at a stop-light on a road in suboptimal driving conditions, or when it's accompanied by the sound of a honking horn and a pair of high-beams embedding themselves in your driver-side window frame three inches from your head. About the only good thing that can come out of a sound like that is the relief when you realize the truck hadn't been going fast enough to actually push you out of the driver's seat.

But the local cops don't see it that way when they get a look at your out-of-state license, which is why they had me leaning against their car while they took my statement, debating whether they should charge me with reckless endangerment.

"You know that it's against the law to drive so fast that you put other people in danger, don't you?" Officer Bellman said. He was easily the more senior of the two, in his mid forties and none-too-happy to be out on a day like this. Up here, they called places like Vancouver and Tacoma "cities," and this guy had the big-fish/small-pond thing going behind the coffee-stained breath that he insisted on sharing with me.

"What part of 'He lost control and damn near killed me' doesn't compute?"

He hitched his belt up, spread his legs a little apart, and swaggered up so he was close enough to kiss me. I resisted making the obvious joke. "I've got you on misdemeanor endangerment, buster, this ain't the time to go pissing me off."

"Look," I put my hands between my butt and the car so I wouldn't be tempted to shove him off me, "I don'tactually think you're an idiot. But it's cold out, and your breath says you've only had one pot of coffee today. I'm just saying you need more antifreeze if you're going to expect your brain to work out in this weather."

"That's it. Turn around and spread 'em."

I shrugged and did what he said. Yeah, I know it's dumb to antagonize the cops, but at that point I didn't give a damn. At that point, I was getting a kick out of the fantasy of suing this joker for false arrest just so I could be the cherry on top of his Sunday the same way he was currently dolloping whipped turds on top of mine.

So, there I was in the klink, waiting for my kid brother Sam—who should have been called Smeagol—to show up and post for me. Then I'd have to stay in over the holiday until the arraignment on Tuesday. Christmas with this branch of the family? Even Dante never thought of that one.

I ground my teeth together. It should have been a nice day of getting slowly sodomized by the gods of Seattle traffic. Rachael had called this morning to tell that there was a problem with Southland, and it was no good going into it on the phone because they wouldn't settle for dealing with my assistant, no matter what. No, they wouldn't talk on the phone. Yes, it had to be in person. No, she didn't have any other details.

Which meant I couldn't wait for the airport to open back up, so I'd rented a subcompact and tried heading south on my own. A thirteen hour drive in good weather, so I'd probably get home about the time the weather broke and I could fly down in two hours, but at least I wouldn't be sitting around the bloody Airport Hilton cooling my heels. I'd comforted myself with the knowledge that at least the conference netted me a handful of leads for regular insurance gigs. Steady work is the unicorn of the self-employed, and there ain't a one of us who's virginal in any sense.

Sam showed up before Manny could find his way back to the land of the wakeful. Just as well—I didn't fancy trying to convince him he needed to buy me flowers before we got serious about our enforced cohabitation.

But Sam I hadn't seen in ten years, and I can't say they sat well on him. He was standing in the waiting area past the checkpoint in the front office. An couple inches taller than me at six three, thin like a toothpick that hadn't been eating properly. At about thirty-two he was three years younger, and he had smoker's lines starting to come in around his eyes and jawline. Last time I saw him was before his wedding. Now he looked like someone who spent a good part of his time playing chewing tobacco to Lady Luck.

"Clarke." He nodded, but barely. Didn't stick out a hand, but he did carry one of my bags. It was more sociable than I expected.

"Sam." I returned the nod.

A banker in the day time for one of those little

independent banks that customers run to when the big banks fail, his Bentley said money almost as much as his house did—a house that took us an hour and a half to find in the ice and snow-covered hill maze.

No chauffeur, which half-surprised me. He set the bags in the back seat and flipped an effete hand to the passenger door, then shambled around to his side, crouching, on the edge of a flinch, like someone used to being hunted. Not the same guy who'd thrown me out of his life once upon a time—on the upside, at least he came and bailed me out.

We didn't slip-slide all over the road—snow tires. Said he kept a spare set in the garage for days like this. He seemed to know which roads to drive to avoid the idiots.

"You still with Oakland?"

He was still on speaking terms with our parents, so he should have known better. Cheap jab. I played it straight. "No. Private now."

"Hmph. Interesting work?"

"Keeps me busy."

"Hmph." Aside from a little bit of the perfunctory tour-guide routine, he didn't say anything much for the rest of the drive. Then again, we'd said all there was to say twelve years ago.

"Well, here we are." He squeezed it out of a tight throat, like he was constipated and trying to get things moving. "Built in the twenties. Three governors lived here after they retired."

"Peachy."

The house was Gothic Revival—high pitched roofs, big lawn, hill, winding drive, nasty-looking wrought-iron gates. The kind of place you might seen in a costume drama, or a Rocky Horror remake, all buried in white.

The reception inside the house was slightly less chilly. I guess upper class manners demand a hell of a hospitality act.

He had me set my things in the foyer, then showed me personally to the dining room where the family seemed to just be finishing up with dinner.

"Clarke!" Samantha—yes, Sam's wife was also called Sam; my brother came up short in a lot of areas, but height and narcissism were two in which he measured up well enough to make a try for the record books—welcomed me with a just-barely-too-warm hug that, along with her parents sitting indifferently at the other end of the long table, made it painfully easy to remember why I hadn't been invited to the wedding. She broke the hug and held on to my arms for a minute, looking at me as if she were trying to see whether I'd changed at all, and in what direction.

Her face was all smiles, but her eyes had a hint of the same hunted look I saw on my brother.

She turned to the rest of the table. "Mom, Dad, you remember Clarke."

Her father grunted a perfunctory greeting. Her mother showed a tad more hospitality, but only as far as etiquette demanded. There are some people who serve as the perfect moral barometer: if they approve of you, it's time to do some serious soul searching.

"Tom. Edith. Good to see you're doing well." I nodded to each of them and smiled a bit, not insincerely. If they were still alive, it went a long way to explaining Sam's bearing.

I turned my attention to the three kids—twin twelve-year-old boys, the product of Samantha's youthful rebellion against the silver handcuffs she'd been born into, and a younger girl, nine or ten if memory served. Even if the trademark pokey ears didn't mark her out as a Lantham, the way she fidgeted under the burden of formality certainly did. "Let's see if I remember." I made a show of squinting hard to remember, "Jimmy, who hates chocolate, Albert, who loves peas, and...Sarah," I looked at her plate, "Who can't stand potatoes."

The boys weren't very impressed, but Sarah seemed to appreciate that someone noticed her. That figured. Sam might be aging fast, but he hadn't changed much otherwise.

"Who are you?" she asked, all narrow eyes and suspicion like she was having trouble placing me on the friend/foe graph.

"This is your uncle Clarke from San Francisco," Samantha said.

I managed not to mutter "Oakland." In this part of the world, it was a meaningless distinction—one city, you were a fag, in the other, you were a gangbanger. All things considered, and despite my adventure in prison earlier today, I'd rather be thought light in the loafers than fast on the trigger—not that I expected these kids to have picked up that much fine-grained prejudice yet.

Jimmy said "hi" with a tone of relief that only comes from having endured too much attention from micro-managing grandparents. Albert, already jockeying to be the pack alpha, stood, sized me up, then walked over and offered a hand, which I shook.

"So what do you do in San Francisco?"

"I'm a private detective."

His eyes did a convincing impersonation of saucers. "Like *The Maltese Falcon*?"

"Something like that."

"Caught any serial killers?"

"Honey," Samantha interposed herself between us, "Your uncle Clarke's had a long day, and needs to eat something before you..."

"No, no, that's fine." Damn the fact that it wasn't my house, I've got a thing about kids that are forced into good behavior. "Ask me anything you like, but dinner sounds good."

"You like pheasant?"

"At this point I'd eat a raw rhinoceros."

"Cynthia!" Samantha clapped her hands like she was calling a dog. A maid, probably a grad student and wearing the most genuine smile I'd seen all evening, and followed by the sound of bawdy laughter, poked her head through what turned out to be the kitchen door.

"Yes?"

"Bring a plate for our guest?"

"Certainly, ma'am." She disappeared again.

The dining room was a cherry-wood finished affair with a long, formal table set without a table-cloth. No centerpiece to prevent the diners from seeing each other—judging by the seating arrangements, this was probably so that the kids wouldn't have anything to hide behind while being scrutinized by the adults on the other side of the table. The head was empty, and I was tired enough that my inhibitions were riding pretty thin, so I didn't quite manage to squelch a very childish impulse.

"I wonder if I...no, never mind."

"What?" Samantha asked.

"Well...no, never mind, really, it's stupid."

"We haven't seen you in more than ten years. There aren't any stupid questions." She seemed to mean it, despite the huffs of derision from both her parents and from her husband, still standing in the doorway behind me.

"There's just always something I've wanted to do..."

Without asking permission, mostly because I couldn't have stomached even *more* politeness, I swept up to the head of the table and sat down at the cleared space that my brother would normally have occupied. I perched my elbows on the table and tented my hands, drumming my fingertips against each other. "Thank you all for joining me," I said in my best Boris Karloff, "There has been...a murder."

Childish, yeah. But I couldn't help myself. I stood up again before anyone could say anything, and took a seat down at the ass end of the table in a blank spot next to the kids.

"Wha..." Sam started.

"Nothing. I've just always wanted to do that."

"Whatever." He left the room rather than take his own seat for some dinner.

Once I'd taken the first bite of my asparagus, Albert considered the interrogation officially open, and in between swallows of a very nice Pinot Grigio and nibbles from the unfortunate bird on my plate, he started grilling me about my glamorous life as a private eye. When I didn't make him shut up, the other kids joined in post haste.

You get used to that kind of thing in my job, if not with this level of enthusiasm, so I gave them a Bowdlerized version of last year's New Year's Eve party—enough action and intrigue to get my niece and two nephews excited, hopefully not enough to give them nightmares or spank material. My sister-in-law seemed to approve, and invited me along to help bed the kids down in the family room. Clustered around the hearth, their annual "sleep under the tree and try to catch Santa Claus" tradition. They kept me telling stories for a couple hours before I finally managed to beg off and go back to my room to check my email.

Seemed like a big house for a family of five, even with the parents-in-law and the house staff—three of them, near as I could figure. The guest room where they stuck me was big enough to hold my whole office suite and a small coffee stand. Sam had done alright for himself, and though I found his paranoid tics unsettling, I couldn't bring myself to feel sorry for him. On anyone else it would've looked pitiful. On him, it felt like justice.

Not that I'm one to hold a grudge.

Or get to sleep early. I toodled around emailing contacts from the convention 'til about ten, then opened up the inbox on my email client. The avalanche of emails from Rachel started pouring in. Looked like she'd given up on text messages when I told her I was going on the road—probably didn't want to distract me when I was driving over the ice.

"This is Lantham 911, what's your emergency?" I muttered to myself as I opened the first one.

It read:

Situation escalating. Southland Corp. account, five stores. Inventory losses. Still no joy with earlier problem. Need to revive stakeout, not enough of me to go around. Need referral to separate agency. Advise ASAP.

Short, irritable, and to the point. She was at least dependable.

The second email:

Southland's getting squirrelly.   Demand round-the-clock surv. or referral to subcontractor, or they threaten contract break.   Someone over there is rattled.   Got bead on a couple off-duty cops who could use the extra work.

The following emails were all updates—resumes and contact info for the off-duty cops. Looked like she managed to get it all together over the course of the day.

I dashed off a quick reply:

> *Rachael-*
>
> *Car wreck and legal troubles have me stuck here 'til Tuesday—hoping for weather break Tues afternoon. Everything under control. Southland plan sounds good. Email forms so we can keep everything nice and legal. Phone charged, I'm in range, call if you need anything. Good work.*
>
> *-Lantham*

That killed about a half an hour.

I shut the computer and went to bed, tossed around for about an hour, then gave up and pulled the laptop back up to do a bit of mindless web-surfing.

Only another four hours until I hit my normal bed time.

This ends this sample of
A Ghostly Christmas Present
Find the rest wherever ebooks and paperbacks are sold

ABOUT THE AUTHOR

WHILE *STAR WARS* and *STAR TREK* seeded J. Daniel Sawyer's passion for the unknown, his childhood in academia gave him a deep love of history and an obsession with how the future emerges from the past. This obsession led him through adventures in the film industry, the music industry, venture capital firms in the startup culture of Silicon Valley, and a career creating novels and audiobooks exploring the worlds that assemble themselves in his head.

The author of twenty-four books and innumerable short stories, his travels with bohemians, burners, historians, theologians, and inventors led him eventually to a rural exile where he uses the quiet to write, walk on the beach, and manage a production company that brings innovative stories to the ears of audiences across the world.

For news, updates, and new releases,
sign up for J. Daniel Sawyer's newsletter at www.jdsawyer.net